W

William Rivière was born in 1954 and brought up in Norfolk. After leaving King's College, Cambridge, he spent several years in Venice. Later he worked in Japan and travelled around the Far East, paddling sampans in Sarawak and sailing lateen craft in the Indian Ocean. His prize-winning first novel, WATERCOLOUR SKY, was published in 1990, followed by A VENETIAN THEORY OF HEAVEN, EROS AND PSYCHE, BORNEO FIRE and in 1997, ECHOES OF WAR. He has one son and is married to a painter, and has returned to Italy where he teaches at the University of Urbino.

'He has written the story of a marriage, and of a girl outside the marriage who watches the disintegration with dismay. It is an old theme, and one that recalls Henry James or Ford Madox Ford . . . William Rivière's treatment is as scrupulous as either of those masters might have demanded. He recounts a sentimental education without sentimentality . . . He has an eye for glamour, but an eye that sees through it also'
Allan Massie in the *Scotsman*

'It is modest in tone, very penetrating, the writing seems full of the changing lights that hang over sand, salt marsh and lagoon . . . *Watercolour Sky* and *A Venetian Theory of Heaven* seem to me two of the most quietly distinguished novels published in recent years'
John Bayley in the *Evening Standard*

'Written beautifully, tenderly, its passion a velvet blackness . . . he encircles the dying of one love affair and the flaring of another with amazing chameleon stealth and imagination'
Scotland on Sunday

'Exotic, unforgettable characters people these pages . . . Its resonances of *Anna Karenina* aside, another of the qualities of this book is its sense of utter timelessness and Rivière's painterly, elegiac evocation of Venice . . . Compellingly told, exquisitely drawn'
Sunday Independent (Ireland)

A Venetian Theory of Heaven

WILLIAM RIVIÈRE

SCEPTRE

Frontispiece: *MELENCOLIA* (1514) by Albrecht Dürer

First published in 1992 by Hodder and Stoughton
A division of Hodder Headline PLC
A Sceptre Paperback

10 9 8 7 6 5 4 3 2

British Library Cataloguing in Publication Data

Rivière, William
A Venetian theory of heaven.
I. Title
823[F]

ISBN 0 340 57736 3

Printed and bound in Great Britain by
Clays Ltd, St Ives PLC, Bungay, Suffolk

Hodder and Stoughton
A division of Hodder Headline PLC
338 Euston Road
London NW1 3BH

MELENCOLIA I

"I am as universal as the light . . ."

The Cenci

"Non posso altra figura immaginarmi
o di nud'ombra o di terrestre spoglia,
col più alto pensier . . ."

Michelangelo Buonarroti

One

Amedea Lezze loved it when winter battened on the lagoon, the tourists thinned out, everyone swaddled the geraniums on their balconies in sheets of plastic which shuddered in the wind. Wet weather blew in from the Adriatic. She'd go clambering up her attic stair, then up to the *altana*, the wooden terrace you see on a lot of Venetian roofs, to watch a storm coming and be hit by it.

Some of the *altana* timbers were rotten, serving only to house colonies of woodlice. The rail along one side was only held in place by the stems of honeysuckle that bound it. Amedea would sniff the sea wind. She'd remind herself that she really must get the *altana* repaired, then it could be creosoted, and wasn't fresh creosote in salt air the best smell in the world? Loose shutters would start their cannonade as the wind got up. Down in the ditch of the canal, boat covers would flog. The corrugated plastic roof of a shed would jerk and thump.

The *altana* was where she had often dined with her father and mother on summer nights. Particularly after rain it was the finest place to be, when the sky over Venice was lush with washed colours, the islands of the lagoon lay closer than at other times. As a child, Amedea had whiled away the longueurs of grown-up dinners by feeding the sparrows with breadcrumbs, by listening to the leftover rain dripping from the jasmin arbour, by pretending to slip on the wet planks. Then after dark you could watch for shooting stars. When she was allowed to sleep on a camp-bed up there, lying awake patiently, impatiently, she saw star after star swoop and disappear, or she thought she did.

She grew up; her parents were killed in the same air crash; she was a fairy-tale princess, longed for, envied, bitched about, standing on her palace roof when storms advanced. Slate-coloured clouds would come ashore over the littoral, ravel over the islands and channels. Then in her foreground they would knot and shred past aerials, past tortoise-tile ridges and gullies and slopes. The Venetian chimneys that looked like vast buckets on stalks would begin to moan and shrill. *Pietra d'Istria* lintels and sills would shine whiter and whiter as the storm-light thickened.

Cannaregio was Amedea Lezze's *sestiere*. (Venice is divided into six sixths; not, like merely terrestrial cities, into any number of quarters.) She'd gaze out over it as over her ancestral demesne and love it with exultant pride, love it most recklessly when the useless old ship of the Venetian state sidled and fretted at her warps in this latest gale, might drag an anchor, might break a hawser, might drift . . .

She loved counting the seconds between lightning and thunder, loved to breathe the rain before it fell. Staring out at the squalls on the lagoon was like watching polo. Drubbing hooves would charge across the expanse, beating a scudding patch of black water to welter. As the game changed, ponies and riders would come galloping another way, swerve toward her. Amedea would wait, held up on her house, exposed. Spatters of rain would score dark streaks on the terracotta urns. For a marvellous instant in the battering onset, she could never tell what was wind, what was light, what was water, what was darkness. Then with her arms cuddled about her head, laughing, shivering, she'd bolt for the mansard.

But now it was spring. The cherry blossom was over; she had seen blossom on an apple tree. And she couldn't idle here all day tying jasmin straggles back onto their trellis, she was bidden out to lunch.

Nancy Goncharov gave cocktail parties, gave dinner parties; but this had been *pastasciutta* and salad, hardly a party at all. When it was over, she said to her maid, "Ask Alvise to be ready with the gondola."

"Yes, signora," replied the girl. She knew the old oarsman was ready. She'd seen him bring the Goncharov boat round to the water-steps as he did every fine afternoon. He'd placed the velvet cushions on the seats. He was polishing the brass-work, polishing the black deck.

"And now my dears . . ." Nancy turned her tiny, almost crippled body slightly toward Claudia Glaven sitting at her right hand, then toward Amedea Lezze at her left and Amedea's cousin, her young Ziani cousin, what was her name, she was a student, Francesca, that was right, at *her* left. The white blobs and grey creases of Nancy's face shifted. Her grey hair stirred. Only her nose, that she called her inedibly old potato nose, stayed still. "Shall we . . . ?" Her lipstick crinkled apologetically. "If you will help me . . ."

Nancy Goncharov's two ladies-in-waiting stood up, they each took one of her arms. The Ziani girl – bad luck or bad management, that voluptuous outline, she'd be matronly at thirty – scraped her chair back. The friendship of Claudia and Amedea, those two women forty or fifty years younger than her, was one of Nancy's cardinal pleasures, dying alone in her palace. She liked the way that when they came to lunch or to dinner they took pleasure from the canvases by Duchamp and Picasso that hung in her dining-room, but didn't talk fulsomely about her paintings. Also she liked the way they winked at her when to amuse new guests she switched on the lights in the hollowed-out cake model of her palace that the chef at the Gritti had made in honour of her last birthday. Hers wasn't much of a palace, because the first owner had run out of money after the ground floor had been built. And it looked even more odd made of cake, sitting on a drawing-room table. Claudia and Amedea were charming, she thought, to go on being amused by the chef's careful wiring, and not to give the joke away.

Gingerly they inched her along the hall. After five minutes, she was resting on a marble bench on the terrace, waiting for her joints to hurt less.

Signor Alvise's nose was different from his mistress's, it was a hooked saw. Only once, when she was being interviewed by the *Tatler* or *Paris Match* or something, Nancy had declined his services for one day. She had had herself photographed being rowed by her maid's lover, who was twenty-three and beautiful. Such were Signora Goncharov's late wisps of humour and vanity. She'd been photographed by Man Ray when she was young: lamé and feathers, a diamond necklace, a long cigarette holder. She still wore her rings of those days – couldn't get them off.

When she had rested, the old gondolier lifted her in his arms, stepped on board, set her down in her chair.

So away we go! thought Francesca Ziani, who was penniless, who had been brought up in a rented house in a suburb on the mainland, who had never been rowed by a paid oarsman before. Away from Nancy's stunted palace. Away from Ralph Chedgrave's house nearby where Claudia lived, Ca' Zante with its Byzantine arches, porphyry roundels, cracked entablature, cracked sills, Lombardo's conception still on its feet after five hundred years but a bit lop-sided now.

Nancy had Amedea sit beside her in the stern – no doubt because she wants to ask if the rumours about Gérard and me are true, Francesca thought, and felt queasy. Amedea who when she was a girl wore her black hair about as carefully as Medusa wore her snakes, but had it bobbed the year before she became a fashionable wife. Amedea who used her grey eyes like two deposit accounts that she could draw on whenever she wanted to indulge herself or make an effect – yes, just like she used her funds in Rome, Geneva, Jersey, her cousin thought. Amedea who ate like a jockey, would always look like one of Modigliani's girls. Amedea who right now was leaning toward her hostess's ear, who right now was probably elaborating on Francesca's, what would she call it, infatuation, damn her . . .

"How is Ralph?" Francesca made herself ask Claudia Glaven beside her in the gondola's bow. Claudia had alarmed her for six months now – ever since Francesca had started at Venice university; had by her cousin been offered a maid's bedroom upstairs in the Lezze house near the church of the Miracoli; had with Amedea and Amedea's often daunting friends begun to patch together a more debilitating education, but more tantalising too, than the university gave.

"How is Ralph?" That Anglo-Irish drawl converted into an Italian drawl quite beautifully, Francesca had to allow, waiting nervously for what sallies – so outrageous one honestly ought not to laugh at them – the stretched, stretched, just beginning to tear syllables might mean. But not today. It seemed Claudia Glaven was in a gentle mood. Though the news was shocking, it wasn't told to shock. Ralph's diet of champagne and cocaine was more often brandy and heroin these days. His rock music business got along better the less time he spent pretending to direct it. His boyfriends were less and less often people one might wish to listen to as well as look at or touch. Where was he now? New York, Claudia thought, but she wasn't sure.

Wisteria furled along a wall was in flower, so was a lilac bush by a courtyard gate. Where the backwaters were quiet, water-boatmen skittered on the glazed calm with their long, starveling, outrigger legs. Canal sunlight rose in furbelows up the honey-coloured house walls, frilled and flounced the arch of a bridge over the Goncharov gondola swaying by. At the corners of canals, Signor Alvise would ask, "Which way, signora?" and Nancy would tell him, or very slightly lift her right or left hand. Being rowed was like what her grandmother used to call "carriage exercise", Claudia said amiably to the gauche girl at her side, recalling the Austins and dog-carts of County Clare.

And Francesca nearly relaxed enough to enjoy it, very nearly. I'm trying hard, she swore to the flies crawling on the paintless gunwhale of a moored barge. When an arm flung a lightbulb out of a window and it smashed against the opposite wall and fell spangling past their heads she jumped – that was silly. But when Amedea called up that they weren't the goddamned rubbish barge, she laughed. And when she saw a bag come bobbing alongside, a bag that could only that minute have been lobbed into the canal because the litter of kittens in it was still drowning, like a Turk in a sack in the Bosporus, she swallowed stalwartly and looked away sensibly and managed not to say a word, not catch anyone's eye even – though this effort was wasted she realised when she heard the gruff voices of the other women on board: "Poor little brutes!" "God aren't people foul?" "But what else can they do?"

Then Amedea Lezze cried, "Claudia, Francesca, do you remember Inez Rivac's wedding?" So Francesca knew her cousin had indeed been murmuring about love affairs and marriages in Nancy Goncharov's ear where the rubies were cobwebbed by ashen hair from her nape, the grey lobes trembled feebly on her mohair coat collar when she tried to turn her head.

Amedea was laughing, one jewelled hand on Nancy's seized-up knee. "Weren't you at Inez' wedding either? In London, about five years ago. She was English for a while." Amedea had a pantheon of friends suitable for most eventualities. Some were pure spirit; all could always be invoked. Was Inez Rivac one of the substantial or conjectural deities? Francesca wondered. There were others she was unsure about too. Luca and Angelica Baldeschi – were they real? And Carl Somebody who lived in Lausanne? Why did they never telephone the house when she was there? "The usual Mayfair thing, Nancy. Half the men in the church had been to bed with the bride, the other half with the groom, and of course there were a few overlappers too."

I'd rather be rowing my own boat, Amedea mused indolently in the way of a confident woman being conveyed through Venice on a sunny afternoon in spring. I love the *s'ciopon* my father left me, from which years ago they used to shoot duck. (*S'ciopon* were built to this day with their bows low as if to allow ghostly wildfowlers to train their long duck-guns along the surface of the lagoon.) I love the heavy, battered hull built between the wars. I love her colours that have never changed: black antifouling below the waterline, green paint above. But now, "Those are his windows!" she softly exclaimed to Nancy, and winked at Francesca, because the gondola was gliding along Fondamenta della Misericordia. "That's the attic where Gérard Charry lives."

"Has he got hot water in that place?" Nancy wanted to

know. She was a kind of grand duchess of Bohemia, for half a century had tried to help her people. So she was relieved to hear from the blushing girl in the bow ("I haven't a clue," Amedea had laughed, "You'd better ask Francesca,") that yes, luckily Gérard had hot water – rain through the roof on occasion, but hot water in the tap – so he was all right. She said, for truly the child was innocence itself, one must be kind to her, "My dear, one evening you must bring him to my house for a drink."

No question of it, Amedea would rather have pushed off from her own mooring posts. And it was ridiculous, the way she even managed to love her slimy water-steps. She loved the way her *s'ciopon* lay alongside the façade, with a painter at the bow and a rusty padlock and chain at the stern. Good God, she was getting to love the gaping hole where last year a block of masonry had fallen into the canal – truly, truly they must get that fixed. And indeed, naturally she had noticed how in this reckoning up of her blessings she was picking her way around her husband and son as if they were puddles and she were mincing in satin dancing slippers. But it was good to go down after rain to bail out the skiff, to sit on one gunwhale to tilt the bilges, to lift the floor-boards, to chuck water overboard and clean the boat up a bit. She liked it when other people along the canal were bailing too. It was neighbourly when the sun came out and vessels dried and bargees going by called and made jokes.

Then Nancy Goncharov was leaning ricketily to confide something – what was it? "Amedea darling . . . No need for . . . I mean, what's the point of the cycle of marriages and divorces everyone seems to pursue these days?" Something like that. There were the regular creak of Signor Alvise's oar, the lapping of ripples against planking, then a barge engine, a child's shout. "What's the use? The embrace, then the domestication. A few years later another embrace, rapidly domesticated. Rather boring, don't you feel? Why this vulgar hankering after certainties?" And when, Amedea wondered with only mild irritation as she nodded and smiled at what she thought the old lady was saying, when will Francesca learn to conceal when she's eavesdropping? And isn't nineteen a bit old for puppy fat? Then she heard the end of Nancy's opinion – "you" and "so brilliant" and "other things" – as slapped about by launches' wakes, shot through by gulls' cawings, it came to pieces.

"Well, there's not much risk of my getting divorced," she said cheerfully to Nancy. (But a contract here or there, a sacrament more or less, were not what the mistress of the gondola had been talking about.) "I couldn't want to get married again."

And what did it matter anyhow if Francesca listened? They'd been speaking in English, the girl couldn't have understood much. And what did it matter if one were – she could remember her father's wisp of laughter as he said it, how he tugged his moustaches – disappointed in love? And what did it matter what Nancy thought? Amedea could forgive mankind all its opinions – ah but how depressing, without exception, were points of view! – because Alvise was oaring them out of the city into the lagoon.

When Amedea Lezze thought of herself, it was water-light she thought of. A shimmer in her head: that was the self she recognised. And today it wasn't wet weather blown in from the sea, it was blue weather from the mountains. This afternoon out on the lagoon – she sat up straight, she narrowed her eyes, she squinted into the brackish dazzle and to the far islands to make sure – there was light that would seem to drift in and out of her brain with no hindrance from her skull.

"A little way out into the lagoon!" Amedea begged

Nancy Goncharov blithely, twisting round in her black seat, setting her palm urgently this time on the rusted-fast knee. And the old lady smiled and said, "Alvise, a little way out into the lagoon, please."

They crossed the channel that was choppy as always with boats' wakes, headed out over calm shoal that glittered like tinfoil. Where weed lay close beneath the surface, the tinfoil was emerald and the oar clogged. Staring far to the north over deeps and shallows, over marshes, then over plains, they could see the Dolomites in their snow, so translucent was the air that day. Piles staking channels and withies staking nets cast their shadows on the water. Tern rose up from mud-banks with their shrill cries.

She would rather have been rowing her own *s'ciopon*, but even putting forth into the lagoon in the Goncharov gondola Amedea found her happiness with no difficulty at all. There it spread, all fifty-five thousand hectares of it, lying between the Adriatic and the land. All the lagoon was hers, from the river Sile in the north to the river Brenta in the south. Its disused salt-pans, warehouses, duck-decoys were hers, causeways and jetties and dykes were hers, littoral villages and island villages, woods, swamps, ruins, all were hers to wander to. So were sludgy creeks where only reed-cutters disturbed the curlew. So were inlets rimmed with alder and tamarisk. So were acres of sea lavender where rotting wherries lay, then watch-towers, market gardens, strands.

Her birds of promise were the egret that waded in shallows to feed. If she sculled her *s'ciopon* with no more sound than an oar makes digging and dripping, she could slide close by the egret and they would stay. She supposed that gaunt whiteness of the egret might make them seem birds of death – but not a death one could be alarmed by, or regret. And since she was a child the egret had promised peace, a peace she was always about to inherit out on that lagoon of hers: maybe in the Laguna morta north of Torcello, maybe in the Fondi dei sette morti west of Pellestrina, somewhere . . . Or had she always just inherited her peace a moment before? Perhaps it was ceaselessly vanishing beyond a reedbed, beyond a tan sail, beyond a church tower . . . beyond the *cason*, those gammy-legged and ricked-backed huts the fishermen perched on stilts here and there on glimmering shoals.

The thing was to get away from buildings and from people. Even though on the lagoon you could nowhere get truly free from ruins and graves, even though half these swamps had been settlements in the last millennium . . . Still, there were stretches of water and marsh that couldn't have altered much since the first fugitives from mainland fighting and pillage escaped there to make a living out of clay and fish and salt.

And the other thing . . . If you were rowing on that wide water under that wide sky – and even if you were being rowed by old Alvise and the others were chattering – the vital thing was to carry your head high and still. Sometimes then Amedea's mind felt like a spirit-level. (She had never told this to anyone. She was thinking of telling it to Gérard Charry, whom that spring she had been teaching to row in the Venetian manner. So when you marry Francesca you can row her about, she would say, and laugh. Gérard would smile wryly and glance away.) But it was true – if Amedea bore her mind carefully in its bone urn out into that blueness, that rippling, that clarity, the spirit-level showed a perfect evenness never known at other places and other times. There was a balance in her head that she caught and lost and caught again.

When the gondola, on its way back to Nancy Goncharov's palace, put Amedea and Francesca ashore at the Lezze house near the Miracoli, Amedea's husband Guy Ashmanhaugh said, "I bumped into Gérard in Santo Stefano, so I asked him to dinner. He said he'd come."

"A party!" his wife proclaimed, striding toward the

telephone. Whom should she rout out? "After dinner we'll roll back the rugs and dance."

Ah that is typical of Guy! Francesca Ziani's composure was put as swiftly, decisively out of action as Corrado's helicopter which he had just stepped back on to so its tiny grey plastic propellers had to be clutched in one hand and the sorry fusilage in the other; so tears clogged his throat when he cried "Papa! It won't fly!" and he had to be picked up by his father (his mother had lifted the telephone); and a tube of glue was fetched by Signora Donatella, who had been Amedea's nanny and was her son's now.

Atrocious! Francesca wailed, her cheeks blanching, her fingers trembling as she held the tube of glue up to the light to read the instructions because old Donatella had left her spectacles somewhere. Ah cruel beyond forgiveness – but on whose part? – that Guy should make a point of inviting Gérard to the house . . . for there were whisperings about Venice that these rowing lessons were not as innocuous as all that. Cruel but typical. As intrinsic to Guy as his height, his slight stoop, the way his brown forelock flopped on his forehead (he was nearly forty, it was freaked with grey), his blue eyes excellent for winking with. Oh yes, when Amedea had gone in for an English husband she had insisted on conventional English good looks.

Of course she had always been going to marry a foreigner, Francesca thought as she mixed the glue. If Amedea had been Paraguyan she would have married a Czech. Francesca supposed that even if you lived where you were born – and Amedea had never been going to live anywhere but her lagoon, God no! – to marry a foreigner was a way of standing at an oblique angle to your society, wasn't it? That being Venetian she had married an Englishman whose forebears had administered tracts of India should perhaps be put down to her snobbery as much as to anything else. Yes, yes, Francesca knew she was being malicious, but she had glue on her fingers. Like Amedea's father had used to have his suits made in London – though that had been normal enough in his set. If she'd had a dog, she'd have had an English breed of dog. As it was she drank Scotch till she discovered Irish.

Francesca tried to hold the propellers against the top of the helicopter steadily enough for the glue to stick. Guy held Corrado close so he could watch. "You'll have to wait till it's dry," she told the child, who was already reaching out, who would break it again, of course he would. But how could she tell his father that she didn't want Gérard invited to the house for her sake? With wobbling gluey fingers, uppity blood in her cheeks, voice as if she had a sore throat, how? She was young, she knew, she was ignorant, she knew. But she was learning – what? That one never knew if one were having a love affair or not – for Gérard and she had become lovers one night, and then had not seen each other for nearly a week, and then there had been a party and a night and a day and a night and then nothing again – and now he was coming to dinner and her fingers were all thumbs and really she wished he wasn't – and of course it was best always to assume you were *not* having a love affair, dear God no, nothing resembling such a, such an absurdity – and . . . "I'm afraid the propellers won't turn any more."

Thus flustered Francesca grieved.

Well, somebody ought to grieve with Guy, she thought at dinner. Not that she could tell if he were grieving.

Immaculate, his good manners. ("British Indian," he had once explained to her apologetically. "Far more old-fashioned than anything you get in England these days.") But something cold, was there, in his determination that none of his guests should have to give a thought to his unhappiness? No, that was pretty ungenerous of her.

Francesca watched Guy at the head of the table, listening to his left, laughing to his right. Was there compassion for him among his friends, compassion because his wife was no longer in love with him, would surely take a lover one day if she hadn't already done so? In the painters, compassion? In Etienne Maas who painted women, usually nudes? In Franco Tagliapietra who painted skies, canvas after canvas of lagoon sunshine and opening heights windswept or still, light after light with their warmths and coldnesses? Compassion in them?

As months went by, Francesca was beginning to find the painters less daunting. She was getting accustomed to how they took turns to try to seduce her. There was a third painter, but he wasn't here tonight. He was Belgian – no, Dutch – no, she was almost certain he came from Luxemburg. And it was disgraceful, disgraceful, Francesca berated herself, to be so muddle-headed, disgraceful not to find out where people came from and then remember. Anyhow he painted bloodshed. And he was just as rotund as Etienne and Franco. And he would take his turn laying siege to her for a week or two while the others were recouping their enthusiasm. For they would advance again, the blandishments would start again. Was it that voluptuousness, Francesca meditated, called especially sweetly to rotundity? Was that why her Boucher figure – ah hell, she might flatter herself once in a while mightn't she? – was forever having to be hugged to those bosoms little less splendid than her own but stockaded with pockets of pencils? For that matter, were taut button-holes necessary to draughtsmanship? At least she was getting the knack of deserting the painters in bars while they drank and drank, because if she didn't get to bed by midnight once in a while she drowsed through her lectures. But she couldn't tell if Etienne and Franco felt sorrow for Guy. She was afraid everyone around the dining table had seen too many marriages become mere formalities. But why was it incumbent on one to seem not to notice?

And what about Cecilia Zancana with her black ringlets and her enviably inexhaustible merriment . . . Any real affection for the master of the house? Cecilia who had been Gérard's lover off and on for years apparently – was that past now? Francesca had to try hard not to long too vehemently for it to be past – when she was down from Como where her father had a factory, no, several factories Francesca had heard, and she had a fiancé. And what about Claudia Glaven, and Gérard himself . . . ?

For second after second, Francesca gazed across the table (the fruit was being passed round, the candles were encrusting their sticks) at Gérard. She couldn't see him. Above his shirt and below his crop of hair, neither of which she saw the colour of, his face was a blank. So uncertain about everything was she, that her bewildered gaze unmade what it looked at, there was nothing there.

There's adoration for you, Amedea Lezze mused, lighting a cigarette, saying No, she didn't want any fruit thank you.

If Gérard had an iota of sense he . . . And I shall buy them a flat, she thought – because of course neither of them had a shilling. Yes, it would be delightful. She would give them a flat.

Gérard took an orange, glanced her way. Keeping her mouth still, she smiled at him with her eyes.

The man peeling an orange, the man whose face had been dispelled by the intensity of doubt in a young woman's look, had grown up in Paris in a house which regarded its avenue through those so-called Venetian blinds you never see in Venice. During his infancy his mother, by dint of spending each year still more of her husband's salary on clothes and make-up, had contrived to endure their suburb. But then a particularly fetching dress, or possibly the skilful way she had trained her stiletto heels to bear her through a party, caused her to become the chatelaine of a mansion in the state of Quebec and of an array of hills and rivers round it.

It was perhaps a shame that the house, for all its truly remarkable cubic capacity, was without charm, and that the acres, for all their stunning number, were not in Provence, but Gérard's mother set herself to make the best of things. She performed her adapting so successfully that when after a year she recrossed the Atlantic for a visit her small son hardly recognised her. The Canadian magnate had turned out to be a man of advanced views; and she, who had once been a tittivated star of plush and adulterous outskirts, now appeared with flat shoes, fawn jerseys and a scrubbed face, ate yoghurt, drank apple juice, didn't smoke, talked about the environment. Unfortunately in time it transpired that the owner of so much of the environment which Gérard's mother had talked about had never married her, indeed was about to marry someone else. So for the last ten years she had been living in a Quebec suburb. She had taken up pottery; she helped run an amateur theatre company; she went once a week to a psychotherapist, which the magnate still paid for.

Gérard's father, having as a young man learned how to stand every page he wrote on a solid pedestal of footnotes – thus elevated, how could his ideas fall over? it was impossible! – was a professor at one of the Parisian universities. Perhaps this was why Gérard had dawdled into academic work – because although the avenue had been depressing to grow up in, he was fond of his abandoned father whose books nobody read. Not that Gérard was particularly bad at academic work any more than he was particularly good at it. By his late twenties he had written various papers in much the same way that he had had various affairs with women: in both cases he was always sincere, never profound.

And now in Venice he gave his seminars conscientiously, walking along the quays to his faculty to do so, a tall lank figure in a shabby loden coat, a figure with lackadaisical arms and legs (but Francesca Ziani had not been the only girl hurrying to a lecture to turn her head), with a bony skull, blond hair, greeny grey eyes.

And now at dinner in the Lezze house near the church of the Miracoli he was embarrassed by Francesca staring at him across the table, perturbed by Amedea smiling at him – was it a smile? – down its bread-littered length, so he made himself finish peeling his orange, start to eat it.

But Anthony! Yes, of course, Anthony! Francesca's heart shouted in relief as she heaved her thought, which was heavy with agitation – and this blindness, where had it come from? – away from Gérard Charry, flung it cascading every-which-way all over Anthony Holt sitting beside her.

Anthony would understand. Anthony wasn't daunting. Not daunting like Claudia Glaven had happily that afternoon in the gondola chanced not to be, but often was . . . Like now, for instance, Francesca was relieved she was several places away from Claudia, because with her brandy in one hand and her cigarette in the other she had cocked one leg on the table. It was an elegant leg, and it made the glasses and elbows and ashtrays and hands around it look dull.

Anthony was Corrado's godfather (the heir to the Lezze fortune was asleep upstairs), Anthony would grieve. Anthony Holt who collected stage memoirs, costumes, photographs, collected letters by Maria Callas, Isadora Duncan, La Duse. Who bought old Venetian books and books about Venice. Who in the morning slept – except on days of exceptional devotion or insomnia, when he attended mass at the basilica. Who in the afternoon read. Who at night in his linen suits and his bow-ties, with his quick light tread which made him glide so his trilby in winter and his panama in summer were always at exactly the same level above the paving stones, was as regular in his movements about Venice as the tides, as he proceeded between his favourite restaurants and bars. More regular in fact, lagoon eddies being less easy to predict than the open sea.

Anthony Holt had shared a season ticket for the opera at La Fenice with Guy Ashmanhaugh, until the latter married and so of course used Amedea's box. And he is as wretched for Guy as I am, thought Francesca. Look how he's stood up from the table, fretted as far as the balcony, lit a cigarette, fretted back to pretend to read the titles in that bookcase. Now he's standing in front of the big looking-glass with its gilt curlicues, fidgeting with his bow-tie. Or is he glancing at his reflected watch – his fingers tweaking, smoothing the silk under his chin, trying to resist the temptation to twitch it undone, start afresh – because his nightly round of cafés has been thrown into disarray by this unexpected dinner party, and what he really wants is to make a dash for the Bar al Teatro before it shuts, then stroll on to the Ala or the Girasole?

But then Francesca decided that the failure of love between man and woman, which ever since last autumn when she had moved into the house at the Miracoli had seemed a failure of the spirit as miserable as the abandonment of work on the Tower of Babel just because of a few miscomprehensions, was something she knew nothing about. And anyway Gérard smiled at her as he passed the coffee. And Amedea was on her side, Francesca was almost sure she was. So she gave herself a shake, burnt her lips on her coffee, stood up.

"Anthony," she said, "I think Amedea wants us to dance. Will you help me roll back the rugs?"

Guy Ashmanhaugh's Venetian life had its rituals.

There were things that occurred once a year, like the regattas of the lagoon to which Amedea and he sometimes rowed to watch the racing – regattas at Pellestrina and Malamocco, at Murano and Burano.

Sant'Erasmo was the regatta Guy liked best. It fell at the end of summer, the same day as the harvest festival. One autumn the storms had come early, it had been too rough to race. Nothing for it but to huddle in oilskins beneath the tatterdemalion arbours and tilts, while squalls dashed against the humble, ugly church built early this century. Nothing for it but to chew your scorched octopus, swig your plastic cup of wine before the rain diluted it too much, look out at miles of fresh water lashing down on miles of salt. You never got white horses on the lagoon – white ponies at the grandest they could be called. But it was fine to watch the herd cantering.

Most years the regatta was rowed on calm blue water below a blue and white sky. Enough people came from other islands to eat a creditable quantity of the fish and *polenta* cooked in the square. They moored their craft to the piles along the tideway. They watched the race for boys, rowed in *puparin*, and the race for women, rowed in *mascarete*. In the square, they admired the waggon bearing the handsomest maize and grapes, courgettes and cucumbers. They stood in a ring and clapped the prize-giving. The racing boats all painted different colours, the awnings, the hats, the water-front trees, all looked very pointilliste when the sun was out and then mezzotint when clouds came.

The show all the Venetian painters held at the Colonnette happened once a year too. They hung the paintings on the columns and along the arcade, from below your knees to way above your head. On that evening every summer, Guy and Amedea went to support their friends who were painters. It was always the most amusing show of the year. The painters and the friends of painters ate *pasta e fagioli* milling along the curving colonnade. If you looked up, arches and gutters and window boxes shimmered in the lights that had been rigged to show the pictures.

Then there was painting the boat. Each year toward Christmas, Amedea and he hauled the *s'ciopon* up through the water-gate and laid her on trestles in the hall. Signora Donatella watched them heave. Her chief pride were the *terrazzo* floors. Guy would come on her leaning on her broom, watching sunlight pitch dustily through the windows on to the speckles of crushed and burnished stone – umber, verdegris, aquamarine, pigeon blood. For some reason she was proud too that no floor in the house was dependably flat; she liked to challenge visitors to drop a marble anywhere they liked. Disappointed that her young mistress had not a tennis ball in her possession, Donatella kept a bowl of marbles on the kitchen mantelpiece. She'd hold a glass sphere up to the sun, turn it musingly, discard it, pick up a second, a third. After revolving several colours in the light, she'd find herself satisfied, proceed shuffling to the *salone*. "Look," she had wheezed for years to Amedea's admirers. "Drop this anywhere." And then she would rejoice when the suitor, having obediently cast down the marble she handed him, watched it waver toward one wainscot or another. "Look at that marble go!" She spoke like a trainer schooling a promising thoroughbred. Then her cough, phlegmatic as the barge engines rammed into reverse on the canal below. And lyrically, "Look at it trundle away!" Rumour had it that somewhere on the *piano nobile* was a place where a marble, if thrown down, would roll a short distance and stop. But Donatella had never vouchsafed where this inconceivable stillness lay, though she would claim she had told Guy.

Certainly it seemed utterly natural to the old woman that he, who had been brought up in India, should come from the East to marry her Venetian princess. While husband and wife scraped and sanded the *s'ciopon*, she'd stand weighing in her palm a clutch of her small glass globes. Or she'd transfer one at intervals from her left apron pocket to her right. Like a cricket umpire with pebbles in his pockets, Guy remarked – but neither of his listeners understood.

The hall gate was wrought iron, so even when it was shut and they were working on the boat they could see the brumous afternoon dimming on a few metres of canal. There were square windows either side, but too barred and dirty to admit much light. A nineteenth-century Lezze had installed violet and red panes over the door into the garden – resplendent in summer, elegiac in winter, never any use for seeing by. They painted their skiff in the glimmer of a murky lantern hung from a beam.

The hall had not been painted for a couple of hundred years. Its greens and pinks and whites were almost one colour. The pilasters were chipped. The swags that had been golden could only be discerned if you knew where to look for them. Standing by their upturned hull with paint brushes in their hands, sometimes Guy and Amedea became inspired. They were going to redecorate the whole house, starting then and there with the water-entrance. They walked about, they dripped paint, they invented scheme after scheme, they waved their brushes at the walls.

Guy Ashmanhaugh was an architect. He restored palaces for his living, repaired roofs, made offices, made flats. Often he had longed to devote himself to his wife's house; he had dreamed of a restoration that would change nothing, save everything. One day, they had always said, one day . . . The place wasn't quite falling down. Water came out of about half the taps, and hot water out of two or three. About half the switches would turn on a light. I hope I haven't left it too late, he thought, listening to his wife tell the table about a new way of cooking guinea fowl, noticing that her light-hearted dull speech – "Rosemary!" she rejoiced – no she didn't, that had been another culinary burbling – "Bay leaves!" she trilled – didn't help. It didn't help at all, her vacuity sometimes in company; it didn't make it any easier to live face to face with your lost love, live side by side as man and wife. You could, it appeared, go on being in love with a woman who trilled "Bay leaves!" So Guy turned to Anthony and Francesca, who were laughing as they tugged and baled a Turkestan rug his father-in-law had bought when he was First Secretary in Istambul; he thought how unfair it was Amedea saying the girl was dumpy – with that rich brown hair and those brown eyes and that smile she had charm.

Yes, he hoped he hadn't left it too late . . .

Because – because – oh for God's sake, because there was nothing finer than painting the *s'ciopon* on winter nightfalls. The hall floor had been raised more than once in attempts to keep the place dry, so the ceiling was too low. High tides still came slopping in. That was right: think about boats, floors, tides. The only furniture was a decrepit bench along one wall. They stacked oars on it. Slowly the hall had become a boat-shed. There were usually the spars of some vessel or other slung from the beams that had long ago supported more lanterns or maybe a Muranese chandelier. A black inflatable dinghy with more holes than anyone could be bothered to patch lay saggily beside its rusting outboard engine. Amedea had inherited a cutter along with her house and her *s'ciopon* – she lay in the marina at Sant'Elena – so the yacht's paraphernalia accrued: coils of rope, fenders, buoys, boathooks, sail-bags, jerrycans, boxes of fairleads and shackles and blocks.

It was peaceful working there in the smell of brackish water and paint. When it grew cold and damp, they lit a fire in the fireplace, though you weren't meant to light fires in Venice anymore because of the attempt to have clean air. Amedea smashed packing-cases for kindling. Guy carried logs to the hearth, heaved them on to the flames. The blaze soon illumined the hall, made the lantern seem even grimier. It was a big fireplace, you could have burned a chest-of-drawers. Its capitals had nymphs and satyrs wreathed in vine leaves.

Often Amedea sang. She liked foreign songs – Edith Piaf, Lotte Lenya. And there was a Cole Porter song that she delighted in: *Are you still drinking in your stinking pink palazzo . . .* ? She sang it sitting on the hearth with a glass of wine, flicking her fingers as she pushed sticks into the flames. The winter Corrado was born, his cradle stood near the fire.

Ah too late . . . Or not too late . . .

Goddamnit, in other cities they build for the future, Guy thought with sudden savagery. The future. That idea. Heard of it? But here my colleagues and I patch and convert and degrade. And for what? That coming generations may ogle dead buildings that look just like live ones? So they can be edified by travesties, eke out a survival?

Well, if he couldn't restore his marriage, maybe he'd better try to convert it. But why the hell had Amedea had to come barging in this evening when he'd been reading *Baron Munchausen* to Corrado? Well, they hadn't exactly been reading it. But Corrado liked the pictures . . . The one of the Baron's horse tethered to a steeple for instance. And Guy had explained how the Baron had mistaken the weather-cock for a stump in the Russian snow, had slept through a night's thaw, had woken to find the church revealed, had had to shoot the bridle to bring his steed to earth. But then Amedea had descended upon them. She had stopped Corrado concentrating, stopped him crowing at the Baron's adventures. She had hauled the child into the air, cuddled him, kissed him . . . She always forced her embraces on him, never waited for him to come to her . . . Signora Donatella, sitting peacefully in the nursery armchair, had caught Guy's eye.

And now he would leave the party in the *salone*, go up to check that Corrado in his sleep hadn't kicked his bedclothes off. Donatella would have already checked. But he could lean at the child's window a minute alone.

Other rituals were seasonal. On winter days in an onshore gale, Guy and Amedea tramped along the Lido. After the season, the beach would have been bulldozed into parapets; the cracked and blistered bathing-huts were shut. Clouds of sand were hurled inshore, dimmed the trees at San Nicolò.

They liked to battle their way a thousand or two thousand metres out to sea along the breakwater where spray scended over them and fell back through the boulders. It was exhilarating to stand by the lighthouse that was a last bastion of land with confused rollers breaking all around. It was companionable to trudge back along the mole that quivered underfoot when a big sea hit it, then back along the thunderous empty beach with salt storm making their windward ears ache, a cold storm-cloud sunset over the trees. Twilight was buffeted at the hospital walls, miry gardens turned it brown. Cars and hoardings were scoured with flurrying grit. Salt spume lost speed, lost height, drifted down into leafless avenues. It was cheerful to take the ferry back to Venice, go to a café to eat *frittelle* and drink chocolate. Cheerful, that is, until the suspicion had begun to creep into Guy's performance of his rituals that it might be Amedea and not Francesca whom Gérard Charry was fascinated by.

Down from Corrado's bedroom, he leaned his shoulder against the cold marble of the *salone* mantelpiece. He watched Gérard and Amedea whirl round in each other's arms beneath the chandelier; glanced away to the Angelica Kauffmann portrait of a Lezze lady who, family tradition had it, had known Goethe in Rome; glanced up at the beams of the *soffitto veneziano*, those brown ridges and furrows, like having a ploughed field turned upside-down and poised over a room Guy thought, recalling the sodden arable wastes around a hated English public school. The French windows over the canal stood open to the April night. In the intervals of the dancers' rock-and-roll, he could faintly hear a singer and an accordionist away on the Grand Canal entertaining gondola-loads of tourists, regurgitating Neapolitan sentimentality on to Venetian air. His mind was a place of baffles and muffles – was that it? Was that why the truth never came to him while it was new and true, he was only ever touched by a weakened and distorted echo? Was that why he couldn't say when he'd known Amedea was well up to fobbing her would-be lover off with her young cousin – was that it? – yes, but she was tossing him the girl as bait too, wasn't she? – ah, well up to any stratagem to keep him in her entourage . . . ?

The great thing was not to panic, Guy told himself. But he knew he only rehearsed that because it was the kind of thing he'd been brought up to think. Things will turn out all right if you're sensible – that was his mother's voice. And then suddenly his eyes glistened; he whose projects were published in Europe's best architectural journals, who should certainly not have been unmanned by his delightful wife's passing fancies, flushed with the longing to be a child again. The child who had never yet set foot in England or Italy. The child who on the tea plantation in the Nilgiri Hills had trailed along with the brown men and the water-buffaloes at evening through palms and scrub. The child whose attendant genii had been the ibis and egret and purple heron pecking in the meadows and paddies, who had come to the vast masonry tank and seen the dusk suddenly fill with wings and the robed women descend the stone tiers to wash.

Don't panic. Be sensible. Yes of course. But no action was likely to do much good in an intangible case like this, Guy thought unstoppably, alarm being pumped briskly by his chest up his throat into his head. Against feelings, what could one *do*? Among abstractions, doing wasn't the right thing to do.

Clearly it was not helpful to yearn for childhood and India. And it would be unwise to loll against the mantelpiece much longer, because soon dear old Anthony would come in mercy to tell him about an Ellen Terry letter he'd recently bought, or Claudia or Francesca would in loving kindness ask him to dance.

Amedea's and his rituals had seemed to bind them together, but now . . . The *bacari* for instance. A Venetian *bacaro* wasn't like the chrome and strip-lighting bars you found on the mainland, and in Venice too now. A lot of the finest had been closed or disfigured, but some remained. Guy and Amedea had liked the panelled rooms where you went at noon or at nightfall to meet your friends, to drink *ombre* which were glasses of wine.

There was the Assassini which was cool and dim on sultry days, where oars hung on the walls, where you sat on benches, ate eggs and anchovies. There were dank rooms in the backwaters of Castello and Cannaregio where Guy went to talk boats; where he went nervously, despondently, now he was no longer the only foreign oarsman on the lagoon . . . not that, Guy smiled a bit wanly at the chandelier, Gérard could yet handle a Venetian vessel anything like as dextrously as he could. In those *bacari* you drank thin Cabernet or Tocai out of chipped beakers. The scummed dishes of *bigoli in salsa* and *sarde in saor* fed the flies. You had to eat *nervetti*, chunks of off-white slimy gristle, *milza* which was milt or spleen, *rumegal* which was oesophagus.

But in the Milion you ate decently and you drank like a prince. They had the finest Prosecco from the Valdobbiadene, it went well with their hams and cheeses, with a cuttlefish or an artichoke. The dishes were chalked up in Venetian on a blackboard, and some could be seen on the counter. It was good to go in under the arbour and stand on sawdust on the *terrazzo* floor. You could study the posters to learn what regattas and concerts were coming soon. The Milion had a good social jumble – lawyers and boatmen, shopkeepers and dancers. You could talk to the cook, who was a poet. He had published Venetian verses. The only other poet ever there so far as Guy knew was the Englishman, Clive Mellis, who when he couldn't afford Harry's Bar would stump in with his plastic bags of cabbages and second-hand books, his hair as grey as the cigarette ash that sifted down his greying shirt, trousers held up by broken braces used as a belt, fastened with one of his children's nappy pins. When after some years Guy happened to discover that Mellis had invented a Latin poet to translate, and these poems had been well received in London, he congratulated him. The poet talked half the night about the beauty of his elegies and the illiteracy of critics, and drank several jugs of the Milion's good Merlot. After that, Guy and he would exchange a friendly word sometimes; but mostly the old man would sit alone with a glass of red wine and read Petrarch or Cavalcanti hour by hour. Franco Tagliapietra would show up at the Milion too, after painting skies till the light failed. As his lagoon skies became more luminous and ethereal, he became more substantial, more gentle, more slow. In the disappointing absence of heaven, he made heavens for a living, along with teaching at the art school. I'll make yours for free, he told Guy once. And he did. It arrived one birthday of Guy's, was hung in the house at the Miracoli.

The Do Mori was a good ritual too. In winter the place

smelled of damp dogs and damp jerseys. In summer it smelled of panting dogs and of the bare arms of people who'd been in the sun. All year it smelled of the fresh bread and fish and coffee everyone lugged in from the market trestles and tilts. Then too there were seasonal smells, fennel for a while, or oregano. Guy and Amedea would come out to where the market was being dismantled at midday, hoses sluicing fish guts into runnels. Maybe Gérard would have been at the Do Mori for a glass of Prosecco too, it was a Venetian observance on Saturday mornings, why shouldn't he partake? Guy and Amedea would board the *traghetto* to Santa Sofia, and if Gérard was in the same black *gondolone* being rowed across the Grand Canal, if he laughed and chatted as they crossed the gaily lapping water, while sun dazzled them and gulls screeched and oars splashed – that was how you met your friends in Venice. Gérard too lived in Cannaregio, he had to get back across the water, naturally he took the boat.

What about sleepy afternoons in the reading room at the Marciana library, would Guy come upon Gérard there? (Really it was crazy, Amedea would exclaim to their friends, Guy should have been a professor of philosophy, not an architect. Who else went ferreting through libraries after volumes of metaphysics? She was sure she was the only woman in Venice who regularly came upon her husband with Kant open on his knee.) And what about that one night of the Venetian year, Guy wondered, when friends dine as late at the Bar al Teatro as they can, then take turn and turn about at the theatre portico with cups of coffee and glasses of *grappa* till morning to buy season tickets – would that occasion be profaned? Then to sit with your elbow on the velvet sill of the box, Amedea's elbow beside yours till she caught sight of a friend the other side of the horse-shoe of air and had to wave; to look up at the clock on the ceiling that had told the time over so much of your marriage's music; to hear the orchestra tuning up, discords jumping about in the pit like frogs; to see the house lights go down . . . these were good things.

And recitals in the deconsecrated church of San Leonardo? Films screened on summer nights in Campo de Gheto Novo under the stars, among the trees and the marble wells? Going to the Azienda Agricola to drink their *vino sfuso* and eat *mostardo*? Tying up the skiff at the Pergola along Rio della Sensa to eat lunch under the vine, the boat moored safely at your feet, Corrado crawling with toy cars on the quay? These were all bad bets, rituals of Gérard's part of Cannaregio, Guy had little hope for these.

They would all be civilised about things. Oh, naturally. Civilised about things. What did it mean? Making light of distresses, making light of joys . . . ? Well, better than kicking up a rumpus, Guy supposed. Not that he could have made a fuss about his distresses if he had tried. About the fact that the rituals which bound his spirit seemed to loose Amedea's, for instance. He had become so nearly silent, so nearly immobile, never another shindy would he make. And who ever protested or reasoned or lamented anyone back into love?

Not that Amedea did not love their Venice rituals. She loves them dearly, Guy thought, like she loves Corrado and me. Dearly . . . They are the kind of thing one does with one's husband and child. Civilised about things . . .

It had been odd, he had first known she was no longer in love with him when he had found he couldn't bear to make love with her. Ridiculously squeamish of him, but there you were. If she only loved him dearly, if she might fall in love with someone else, he couldn't want to lay a finger on her. And there she was now under the chandelier, radiant but disengaging herself from Gérard Charry, catching Francesca's sleeve, insisting they dance together now, laughing but insisting, "It's your turn!"

Then rituals that weren't the tissue of Guy's marriage. (Oh God, had it really tattered so badly already? And why couldn't he stop feeling it was going on tearing this evening?

His shoulder shifted nervously against the mantelpiece.) Rituals that were not the warp and woof of anything more solid, more apparent, more identifiable than himself. Just him: Guy Ashmanhaugh. The professional partner of Mauro Zanier, who was a splendid fellow – at lunch time they tended to play chess rather than eat stupefying meals. The father of Corrado Ashmanhaugh aged four. The husband of a wife who had chosen to keep her own surname, not unreasonably since no Italian could pronounce his. Scarcely to be dignified as rituals perhaps, these familiar joys. But . . .

Winter dusks along San Leonardo, where in rabbit-skin hats and loden coats people sold walnuts, hazel nuts, roasted chestnuts, dried apricots and figs. Then when tides rumpled over the quays and as they ebbed left baulks of timber, dead animals and dead birds, plastic bottles, mud. When fogs came . . . Not Milanese peasoupers. Not the murk that will swamp the Arno at Florence for days. But good Venetian *caigo* Guy liked, numinous and white, stealing softly over the islands, through the alleys and waterways. Till the masthead lights on the fishing-boats unloading their catch at Sant'Alvise or at the Misericordia or behind the Gesuiti seemed just the whitest gleams in all the white iridescence around. The men's woollen hats had fuzzy haloes of freezing fog. Winches, gangplanks, rigging, nets, appeared calm and immaterial because fogs only came when there was no wind. When the persimmon trees and all deciduous trees had lost their leaves, persimmons still hung reddish gold from black boughs, and they looked handsome in fog, Guy thought, summoning up his threatened delights, his strengths, himself.

Ghostly presences, too. Colleoni cast in bronze on his bronze high-stepping horse, lording it over Campo San Giovanni e Paolo, as proud and confident as the heart could desire. Why Guy had made a hero of that mounted general he wasn't sure. Perhaps because those jutting armoured heels, that jutting helmet, jutting chin, had all the brazen virtues he lacked. Or something to do with bitterness. Colleoni was just bitter enough to be incorruptible by the world's slow stainings now, he'd got clear away.

And that other presence, which Amedea couldn't see, so he'd never been able to share it with her along the littoral at Malamocco.

When summer came, Amedea and Guy and Corrado would often go to swim off the sea-wall at Malamocco or at the Alberoni off the breakwater. Some of the Malamocco *bacari* were fine places, and Corrado scampered in and out of the kitchens and was made much of. One place had iron tables on gravel and weeds in a glade of bougainvillaea. Another had a restaurant that was a conservatory in a kitchen garden.

The dunes at the Alberoni were the enclave of the pride of Venetian homosexuality, but the breakwater tended to heterosexuality and to fishing. Inshore by the pilot station, you could look south across the lagoon mouth to the churches of San Pietro in Volta and Pellestrina, white façades on blue tideway. They had a friend who was a harbour pilot, and Corrado always waved and shouted "Mario! Mario!" optimistically when a pilot launch went by.

Offshore, tankers waited, fishing-smacks trawled. Lazing on the breakwater, you heard the chug of a mussel-boat, nothing else but the lapping sea. The best time to swim was on a rising tide, then if you dived off the lighthouse boulders the channel was clean. Along the mole stood huts with yard-arms; fishermen lowered nets into the tide and winched them up.

Cobalt sky and earthen sea till evening. Then if they strolled north they saw nuns come out of the nunnery in their white habits and promenade on the beach. People without arms and legs came out of the hospital to sun their stumps. Nurses shoved wheelchairs ponderously over the shingle and sand with those patients whose legs had been recently cut off. It was a hospital which specialised in disfigurements.

Then strolling along the sea-wall, sun setting on eastern sea, on littoral reedbeds and vegetable patches and dykes, setting on western lagoon and islands, Guy saw Dürer's Angel of Melancholy hulked down by the shore. He didn't know why he saw the angel. But she was always there. When there was a pale day moon; when he was carrying Corrado whose bare arms and legs he could feel in his arms, whose salty skin he could breathe, could taste; when he could breathe a bonfire, hear hens cackle going up to roost; gazing toward Malamocco church tower, far reaches of lagoon, a tiny Venice on the horizon, he saw the massy angel every time.

Perhaps it was because of Amedea's mirth at how grave Guy could be . . . Perhaps that was why he'd never tried to make her see what he saw. Anyhow the angel never moved. Elbow on knee, majestic head bowed, there she sat amidst the meadows and outhouses, bramble and sedge, where the first bats would be swooping now. Guy saw the angel's furled wings; her bony dog, a sort of lurcher, asleep; books chucked down in the dust, all the failed attempts, débris of the speculation of centuries, the great adventure that had amused a few people briefly. It was as if from the Renaissance the artist had sent his angelic thinker forward to warn Guy of ignorance and meaninglessness. (And certainly he should never have become a conservation architect, Amedea would announce. Seeing palaces decay made him gloomy, restoring them made him positively suicidal. Ah, his depressions! Where did they come from?) The Angel of Melancholy had been here at the rebirth, Guy would muse, and seemed to be here at the next death – or had she always haunted here? As if when the glamorous ballet of *a priori* possibility came off after the longest run in theatrical history, when the metaphysicians grew arthritic and fat, the genius who had choreographed the finest dances sat down and grieved. Happened to sit down right there, where Guy often came with friends or alone, then with his wife, later again with his wife and their child. Of course there'd never been any point in asking Amedea if she could see Melancholy. (Too late! a voice whispered. Or not too late . . .) Because Dürer's angel on the littoral at dusk was nothing at all, just happened to be a trick of inexistence that made Guy be himself – more than a regatta that was first pointilliste, then mezzotint, more than persimmons that hung in freezing mist – a grace that made him, made him be. So, like the angel, he gave no sign. Time after time, he passed by, marvelling.

"I'd like to dance with you," he said.

Because Francesca Ziani beneath the chandelier had quit dancing, had grabbed Claudia Glaven's elbow, had chittered "It can't be let go on, it can't, Guy's been propped against that mantelpiece not smiling for half an hour." The portly painters had mopped their foreheads with handkerchiefs. Claudia had replied curtly (dear God the girl could be young!) "Ten minutes;" and had drawled, "He's all right." But by then Francesca had planted herself four-square, arms akimbo before him and demanded, "Do you want to dance with Amedea or Claudia, or will I do?"

Did it matter if Amedea taught Gérard to row the *s'ciopon*? Guy wondered after midnight when the dancing had stopped (certainly her dancing with him gaily, sweetly, hadn't mattered a jot), and Anthony was flicking through records, looking for something for them to listen to since no one wanted to go to bed, and anyhow the wind was getting up; in their arches the French windows were swinging and creaking; then blustery rain swished down.

True, the first time Guy had strolled home from his studio and seen the skiff was not moored by the water-gate, he had been as astounded as if the boat had lain there but the house had after three centuries upped and offed. Then he had thought the boat had been stolen. Then he had realised.

Whose heart would not have protested? Ah Amedea couldn't we have kept rowing the *s'ciopon* to ourselves? Can't our evenings on the canals be a ritual just for you and the child and me? When commercial vessels give up and the city's backwaters are still and shadows fall, all I want to do ever is scull with you slowly, softly, past water-steps and colonnades, under decaying bridges, by vines reefed along walls. Goddamnit I asked you to marry me on board that boat. I sat on the thwart with the sun in my eyes and my wrists slacked over my knees only not a nerve in me was slack and you said Yes and went sculling fluently on till in anguish I stood up to kiss you and the boat starting rocking like mad and you remarked that it would be a good idea if we sat down. We even rowed away from our wedding – because you declared you weren't having any of that bourgeois toing and froing in a hired gondola, not even in Nancy's, she'd offered us hers, with two dolled-up oarsmen, with bouquets sprouting out of black paint. Amedea Lezze rowing in her wedding dress, that enchanted Venice all right, that was in the papers next day. I enjoyed that bit, rowing away escorted by a flotilla of friends. I hadn't enjoyed the church. Your contempt for Christianity is such, I don't think it occurred to you that maybe a faith shouldn't be exploited just for your airs and graces. You wanted plenty of fanfare, and you got it. I'd rather have married you at the Municipio. I remember thinking all that lying pomp was how lovers were mildly corrupted even on their wedding days. How children were signed with the potter's thumb of perjury even before they were conceived.

Ah to hell with it. There was no harm in Gérard Charry – how could one think there was? He had come out in the *s'ciopon* with them once, as dozens of people had. He had remarked that he'd like to learn to row one day. Amedea had said she would teach him. He had said thank you. Yet it would be better if Francesca were prised away from Gérard, even at the cost of a nineteen-year-old broken heart which would mend. Yet you couldn't help liking him, with that hay stubble on his head, with those arms and legs he left lying around his chair. Yet Francesca should not have him. For fear of Amedea's machinations, she should not. Yet the girl had been poring over a Parisian journal one evening, just because it had a poem of Gérard's in it. She had gone to the French faculty, found it, one of those literary magazines, brought it home. Yet Gérard had had that futile affair with Cecilia, you couldn't trust him. Yes, definitely Francesca must be warned . . . even if it left Amedea and Gérard standing shoulder to shoulder as they were standing now, Amedea saying, "Her name was Marcella Lezze, she knew Goethe in Rome."

So reflected Guy Ashmanhaugh; and said, "Vivaldi would be great," to Anthony Holt. Coolness of the rain blew in from the windows. The silk curtains began to flutter out onto the balcony, back into the room, like giantesses in swirling skirts who couldn't decide to go out or come in. Twelve-foot swags of red and yellow flung themselves out from the cornices, fanning the air, fell back and swept the floor, then rose again. None of the listeners to the music spoke. Where had old Donatella got to this evening? Guy started drowsily. Usually she joined them for dinner; or if she didn't want to do that, she came in for a few minutes to talk. Guy and Donatella were allies. It had never made any difference that his fellow countrymen had killed her husband at the Battle of Matapan, a Venetian seaman old enough to shave alternate days, gone down with his ship in the fighting that Mediterranean spring night. But now where had the old woman vanished to? Was it something in the air . . . ? Guy wondered, who in a promiscuous society was a natural monogamist. Was it Gérard's presence she disapproved of?

Then Guy forgot everything while he listened to the Vivaldi, and when it was over he reflected that he couldn't be very sharply afraid of anything if he could still enjoy music untaintedly like that. Still, something underlay the Vivaldi – what was it? India! Of course. He was sleepy. But India . . . ? As a boy he had longed for Italian churches and palaces. He remembered begging his mother to let him continue at the mission school in Mysore instead of dispatching him to England. That way – he'd worked it out, he showed her his jottings, his sums – they could afford a month in Europe each year, oh easily, six weeks, to visit castles, cathedrals, châteaux. And when she took him to Calcutta and they saw the Victoria Memorial, he knew that when he grew up he would live in Venice, he'd have to, because if his recollection of the photographs in the book at home in the Nilgiri Hills was reliable, the dome by the Hoogli had been inspired by the dome by the Grand Canal. And would his mother indeed have done better to let him go on hacking his pony accompanied by the syce to catch the little train to the mission school? Apart from what would have been the immediate advantage: that he could have come home every half-term, instead of sometimes only one holiday a year. Would the temples of Magna Græcia one year and the Palladian villas the next have stopped him idealising the Mediterranean so unknowingly? Made him less innocent when as an undergraduate he fell in love with Venice and, a few years later, with a Venetian? What bullshit was he thinking?

Amedea was saying, "Gérard, if you like rowing Venetian boats, we could see about having one built for you."

Jolted alert, Guy sipped his glass of wine so it wouldn't look as if he were paying much attention. He heard Gérard muttering about how they must be very expensive; saw him blush, saw his eyes suddenly overjoyed, how in that instant he was realising that a vessel of his own was Amedea's way of giving him – what? – the freedom of her city and her lagoon.

Ah but she was brilliant, Guy thought. Because the next moment he was watching Gérard realise a boat could equally mean that she wasn't going to have much more to do with her cousin's lover, she'd go back to sculling her *s'ciopon* with her husband and son.

Gérard choked, pretended he'd swallowed a mosquito – he'd forgotten it was still spring. And she has me in the same quandary, Guy thought; and sipped his wine (Gérard was gulping his) and wondered collectedly, "We must think what kind of craft Gérard would like."

Amedea was explaining how new boats needn't be that expensive, she knew a yard . . .

Anthony Holt stood up. Hot after dancing, he had undone his bow-tie, it dangled under his chin. He took off his round, gold-rimmed dark glasses and polished them. His mouth seeped cigarette smoke.

"I must . . . I said I'd meet someone at the . . . at the Girasole. No, no, you don't all have to go just because I . . . Awfully interesting, Guy, that Lillian Gish letter I was telling you about, you must come and . . . I know it's early . . . I mean late . . ."

Gérard Charry wanted to be alone. Of course Francesca had been glorious that night after a party when they had come out on to a quay, she had taken his arm, had laid her head on his shoulder, had come back to his attic. But now among the others at the door of the Lezze house, the others all kissing good night, calling thank you, calling good night, he too kissed, he too called.

The rain had blown over, the wind had died. Trees in

the gardens dripped. The clouds were opening, Gérard could see the moon. Light-heartedly he heard his leather soles tap. He would never make any move toward Amedea. It was impossible. She was married to Guy. And she . . . She would either turn toward him one day or she would not. But meanwhile . . . With him making no gesture toward her, with her making no sign to him (but what did this idea of having a boat built mean?) there was a balance between them that he liked. A balance . . . The beam was level, the scales were still.

Guy's way of life was to be envied, no doubt about it, Gérard thought – who did not imagine him now loading dirty plates into the washing-up machine with the desolation of the husband who does not wish to be separated from his son, knows he must therefore allow his wife any coldness, any breaking of promises, any deceit she pleases. And Amedea kept saying he ought to marry Francesca, saying it in that laughing way of hers . . . (In the kitchen at the Miracoli, Guy straightened his stiff back. He would try to have a word with Francesca before she went to bed.)

Far off, San Marco boomed three o'clock. Strolling, Gérard imagined Guy leaving his studio each evening after work. Saw him go with Mauro Zanier to drink an *ombra* maybe. Saw him walk on through the *calli* bright with street lamps, bright with windows, bright with stalls with lanterns, *calli* bustling with people buying things, people going home, people going out to dine. Saw him come back to Amedea . . . (But did not imagine a man whose obscure, magnificent destiny it was to meet the Angel of Melancholy on a littoral at nightfall, to receive from those shoulders, wings, hands, lips the understanding that the humanist endeavour had failed, from that august despair that the transcendental leap had fallen back.) Was that what life with Francesca would be like? Gérard saw himself walking home through streets of shoppers, then turning into a quiet courtyard, coming to a door . . . Of course they'd have to find a decent flat, his attic would never do. But the university might come up with a better job one day. And when Francesca had taken her degree, she would get a job. And he would live all his days in Amedea's circle. That, naturally, was not the point. But all the same. And Francesca really was a glorious person. Had he not used that very word when thinking of her five minutes before? Glorious.

Tomorrow he would ring her up, Gérard resolved, noticing how the lamps in brackets under archways cast spiders' webs of shadow on the ground. And lamp-light on canals shimmered up again out of black mephitic water, left below the drifting bottles and scum, beat slowly up in great swans' wings, pinion after pinion hooping up cracked walls. How silent the city was too, after the bells had echoed away! Gérard forgot Amedea's black bobbed hair and vamp mouth; forgot Francesca's brown hair on his pillow. A drainpipe glugged, with a swoosh debouched froth into the filth below. Then he heard voices behind a shutter. They were baking bread. He stopped to breathe the good smell.

The tide was going down. One of the vessels moored along a canal had snagged her warp, the hull was cocked up on one gunwhale, when the next tide came she'd fill. Gérard climbed over the iron rail, hung on with one hand, heaved at the slimy hull with the other. He braced a foot against the quay, he wedged the other knee under the rubbing-strake, he shoved. He was yawning, this was ridiculous. His head swam. He'd be crouching there till dawn, he'd have to give up. Then with a crash of waters the boat fell. Gérard thought he heard the roar of time cascading through the splintered flood-gates of the minutes and years in formless ruin. No he didn't. He'd probably just drunk too much wine.

Coming toward his flat along the Misericordia, he thought the bells of San Marziale in their belfry looked like vast, bronze, squat bats hanged by their heels – only at night they didn't kick into flight. He stood still. And then he felt time take the world from him into the beginning of its obliteration. His heart thumped, his eyes dripped, second after second slid from his mind and took the whole world with it into vacuity. Of course he'd thought about transience before – but he'd never felt it, felt how beneficent it is, felt how it makes us free. Never before had he trembled with happiness at how mercifully the burden of old meanings, old lies and truths, old wrongs and rights was lifted from the tiny portion of all thinking that he carried in his skull.

He gasped, shook his head, wiped his cuff over his eyes, couldn't help smiling in a quivery way. So this was it. No wonder he'd never known how to fall in love. So . . . no holding close, no holding fast. So . . . you opened your arms, you let go, let vanish away. Gérard took a slow step on the quay. A second, a third, hesitantly. And momently a new world came . . . There were two equal miracles, there were the going and the coming, this was the second, triumph filled his heart. That night he was blessed with how new each world or instant was that possessed his brain and then disappeared forever, had no being except memory, no truth that didn't change and change and fade away.

He hoiked his key out of his pocket, but then paused outside his front door. The two marble bollards by the water-steps gleamed white. Bags of rubbish lay waiting for the barge that would cart them away in the morning. Gérard's half-written *thèse de l'état* had been toted downstairs in plastic bags one night, left for the rubbish barge. Ever since then, he'd had a particular liking for the *pietra d'Istria* bollards that had presided over his decision that life was too short, and should be made too amusing, for such careerist tip tap retyping. The next morning he had chatted to the boatmen as they hurled his files on board.

But now it was better to be awake than asleep. With these stars coming clear now it was a lot better, and the way the quay and roofs glistened after the rain. In that hush he could stay and never move again. He could sit on the bridge parapet as he often did alone at night and wait for the false dawn, wait for the dawn chorus in the Servi garden behind its red brick wall. Wait with more understanding this time. It didn't matter if one day he married someone like Francesca or he didn't. Waiting for the day's first traffic on the canal, that would be clear. Watching the moored craft lie motionless over their reflections, that would be clear. Watching a rat swim across. The Citroën chevrons it made. Tomorrow he would ring her up. He mustn't forget. Who could tell? Affection and kindness might be theirs. Children might be theirs. Anyway dinner next week couldn't do any harm. While love, if it ever came, would go. Probably Francesca understood this. Probably every living soul in Venice understood this except him. They couldn't all take their affairs and marriages as profoundly as they pretended to, could they? Not even the nineteen-year-old girls. If he ever fell in love he'd stand like this on a quiet quay at night and love would bless him and he would bless love's transience. There would be no whingeing for perpetuity. No grabbing. No. A love affair was honest, honourable, it looked the world in the eye and saw decay. The trick was to renounce with a good grace. Then you didn't befoul things. You were as blessed as it was possible to be. He must remember. When the time came, no, now the time had come, he would stand still like this with his arms slack and his head up and feel it and rejoice in it and let it go.

If he waited enough nights, enough years, maybe his miracle would come again. How had he not wept for such goodness and mercy before? Well, anyhow, if he waited an hour, out at sea the sun would rise to the surface, the grey calm would glow with pinks and golds. Then daybreak would sweep ashore over the ripples, jump the Lido like a water-ski jump, plank down on the lagoon, come swishing ashore at San Marco, ski swishing up the Grand Canal . . . He'd breathe the sea air of a new day. Luxuriously, he swung his heels against the parapet. Luxuriously, he stretched his arms.

No, he must sleep. He would sleep. That was a sensuality too. To take the telephone off the hook, drink a glass of water, undress. To lie on white sheets by an open window. To wake to hear the birds had been singing for hours, the air was bright, was warm, the quay was bustling with voices, with boats. To lie on his back and dream. The sun off the canal would play its daily ripplings on his damp-stained ceiling.

Then he would dress, go out into the smell of sun on water and the smell of ground coffee and the smell of sawn timber from the carpenter's yard. He'd buy *La Repubblica* and a couple of brioches and a litre of milk. He'd stand beneath the awning on Rio dei Ormesini to buy oranges, and hear yet again how the fruitseller had been a champion player of *bocce*, he had ventured to the mainland and won contests there; how it seemed to take a Venetian to bowl with true acumen, to bowl astutely, what did Gérard think?

Barges would be unloading sheet-metal at the foundry. Fishermen would be unloading buckets of eels that writhed slower and slower in their blood-stained slime. In the humble bars, the first glasses of wine would be drunk, dazzling tide lapping flush with the quay outside. Washed sheets would be hauled on pulleys across canals to dry.

Gérard fitted his key in the lock.

On her way to bed, Francesca Ziani was stopped by Guy Ashmanhaugh. "You're being used as a lure," he said gruffly.

"What's a lure?"

"Oh, it's a thing made of feathers to look like a bird. The falconer whirls it around his head, the hawk stoops, comes to his wrist. He feeds it a gobbet of meat, slips the jesses on its legs, puts a hood on its head so it can't see."

Francesca leaned against her bedroom door. She felt as if she'd been kicked in the stomach. Her thoughts wouldn't focus, they wandered off stupidly. Was that how Guy had spent his time in the desert with that rajah friend? Was that jeep they jounced around in full of hawks?

"Either you're the lure," he was saying, "or you're the gobbet of meat."

Two

On spring mornings, the sun's reflection swaying in the dirtiest canal was silver, but too silver to look at. Those were mornings to go afloat. To walk about on the ground could never be commensurate with such light, Amedea Lezze would declare – who as an heiress could fritter away her days as she chose, who had never been ruffled by any wish to be a business woman in order to augment her fortune.

She would drag open her rusty water-gate, step on board her *s'ciopon*. She would fit her *forcola*, the carved wooden upright used on Venetian vessels instead of rowlocks or thole-pins, into the starboard gunwhale. She would push off from her mooring posts that had once been painted in blue and white bands with a gold topknot, but had faded, had been bashed, scraped, chafed. She would pick up her oar . . . All this after kissing Corrado as, escorted by Signora Donatella, he stumped off to his infant school. And sometimes that March, April, May, June, after ringing up Gérard Charry's attic. She had asked him for his university timetable. When a few days later he had neglected to let her have it, with hauteur she had telephoned his faculty, extracted the information from a secretary. On another occasion – truly it was a little disappointing, how spiritless he could be! – he had claimed that there were mornings when, even if he wasn't at the university, he didn't feel free to come rowing, he ought to stay at home and read. She had had to speak quite mockingly to him.

The first day Amedea tried to teach Gérard to row, she embraced his back and leaned around him and laid her hands on the oar beside his. Then she took over the oar and commanded him to embrace her and to try to catch the rhythm like that. They tottered and giggled in the quivering skiff. The slightest ripple had Gérard off balance. He heaved, he jerked. His back and his arms ached. His oar kept falling out of the *forcola*. The mistress of the *s'ciopon* offered to tie it in with a length of cord, "like the fishermen do for their children". He refused indignantly. She offered to kneel at his feet and keep the wayward oar in place with her hands.

Gérard made a stroke over the starboard gunwhale; the bow swung to port, in to the side of the canal. Indolently Amedea fended off. The water was light green in the sun, dark green in the shade. Tumbling midges speckled patches of air. Someone on a high balcony with a watering-can tipped splatters down through the dappled gap between the houses till they splashed onto the *s'ciopon*'s floor-boards. A gondolier called to Gérard with instructions. He struggled to do what he was told. Standing wrong, swinging wrong. Amedea explained, "Don't push and pull your oar. It's a circular motion. Swing up and over and round." Then the boat lurched, Gérard's oar had snagged; he lifted it clear of a bloated, a hairless, a cat probably he decided, but it might have been a terrier.

When Amedea thought her apprentice could steer a straightish course, she let him try to cross the Grand Canal. But he lost what faltering rhythm he had acquired. The *s'ciopon* eddied in anticlockwise circles. A *vaporetto* descended upon them, its passengers pointing and laughing. A post-office launch came one way, a gas company barge the other, both blaring indignant horns. A taxi boat, swerving to avoid Gérard, chucked up a steep wash that slopped on board. The harder he rowed, the more briskly the skiff revolved. If he slackened his efforts, the skiff drifted on the Grand Canal and motorboats hooted and tourists laughed. Then he lost his footing, dropped his oar, crouched, grabbed a gunwhale to stop toppling overboard. Amedea rescued his oar before it floated away.

The next time they went on the canals together, he fell in. He stood up to his shins in ooze and up to his chest in foul water and grinned at her. She hauled him back on board.

Amedea rowed Gérard back to his attic. The house had never looked so dingy, he thought, squelching through the narrow hall past the tide-lines of salt that floods had left on the walls. Why had he never minded before that the entrance had no windows? He dripped muddy water up the mean stairway past the deal doors to other flats. Ushering his unexpected guest to where gullshit encrusted the skylight, he warned her to duck her head, there wasn't a door in the place you could walk through upright.

When Gérard came back from his shower, Amedea was rocking in his rocking-chair. With lazy taps of her expensively shod feet, she pushed at his unswept *terrazzo* floor. Table, bookshelves, everything looked dusty in the sunlight. But seeing her there – the faint stirring of her skirt as she rocked, the faint stirring of her bob (he was sure her hair was inconceivably soft) when she saw him come in and she smiled – Gérard was so happy he had to turn on his heels, hurry to the kitchen for a bottle of wine so he could offer her at least some humble, attic hospitality: anything to let the intoxicated blood suddenly rampant in his cheeks trickle away.

Square mansard windows looked out beneath the eaves down a slope of tortoise-tiles. They leant on the sill with their glasses of wine, Gérard showed Amedea his view. The view was that attic's only charm. Apart from the fact that it was skyed over the finest *fondamenta* in the finest *sestiere* in the most beautiful city in all of beautiful old Europe, he believed.

Gérard pointed out the shabby *squero* where they patched and tarred old vessels, where they beat out iron rails and tin chimney pots. The shed roof sagged like the back of a decrepit horse. The tin chimney which might have attracted custom tilted rustily, kept from falling flat by those of its wire stays that hadn't snapped. Leaning so close beside Amedea's blue shirt with its lace at cuffs and breast and throat, Gérard found the longing to kiss her meant his Italian subjunctives and conditionals knotted in his gullet like bowlines tightening and wouldn't be untied, any verb not regular was a clove-hitch belayed round the cleat of his tongue. They watched a nun in the convent garden where the church of the Servi had been pulled down after the Republic fell. The nun emerged from an arbour where vines were coming into leaf. She wore a gondolier's straw hat with a scarlet riband, and she was driving a rotary digger. She wrenched her iron horse round at the end of a row, trudged behind it back across the vegetable patch. Another nun came out to feed the hens in hutches under a trellised wall. High in the distance, a palace roof was being repaired. A builder wheeled a barrow in silhouette against blue haze.

Gérard was relieved when Amedea said thank you for her apéritif, she must row home now, Corrado would be back for his lunch; but then she lingered. One of the roof cats came to the window. This was a particularly unappealing creature: worms, mange, no tail, a suppurating stub for one ear. Gérard fetched milk from his fridge, set a saucer out on the tiles. The cat lapped its milk; then crouched with quivering haunches to drip its slime.

"I saw a hoopoe fly up from that garden once," Gérard said in the silence.

"A hoopoe!" his guest cried. "In the middle of Venice? How extraordinary! I haven't seen one for years, even on the lagoon. And now honestly I must go." She put down her glass. But then she meandered about the room. Tap of a shoe. Quietness. Then tap, tap. Quiet again. A single tap – her weight shifting from one leg to the other. Then tap, tap, tap, tap, and "Oh look, you've got one of Etienne's drawings too! Rather better than any of ours, I think. You must promise to come and look at them and see if you agree."

As he followed her down the stairs, she stopped, gazed up at him. "You know, I've never looked down into the Servi garden before." Down then half a flight; another stop. "Those bastards, those French, they made Venetian workmen pull down a lot of Venetian sanctuaries. Have you seen pictures of the church that used to stand where that nun was gardening? It was magnificent." Down a few more steps. Then with her smile tilted up, "Oh God, I'm sorry, you're French aren't you?"

And then, it had been strange, on the quay she had dilly-dallied again, Gérard thought when he had watched her row away, when he was going back upstairs. Or rather, not on the quay. Standing in her *s'ciopon*. She had picked up her oar. He had untied her painter. But she had not asked him to cast off, so he had stood holding the rope. And she had stood very slim and straight in her narrow boat, holding her oar idly in one hand, letting it trail. Venice was still a sanctuary, wasn't it? she had demanded. For the place had first been built by fugitives. And later, she had told him, think of all those mainland popes and princes who saw their victims escape to live with dignity on this lagoon. Think of Paolo Sarpi, how he held the Republic together in evil times, think how the pope's ruffians attacked him on a bridge, how they left him for dead, but how he lived, Amedea had said. Sarpi had recovered from his wounds, he had lived, she had repeated, looking away along the *rio* as if for words, looking back at Gérard standing above her on the quay. The bridge where they had attacked Sarpi was just around the corner, probably Gérard knew. And even now – even if the Servi had been pulled down –

a vegetable garden was a sanctuary of a kind, wasn't it? So it seemed to her. Again Amedea had appeared at a loss for words; again she had looked away along the wall between the nunnery garden and the water, looked back into his eyes. Perhaps . . . She had laughed. Perhaps this was why she liked teaching him to row. Apart from him looking so funny. And she was sorry he had fallen in. But . . . He wasn't Venetian, so showing him how to handle lagoon boats – did he understand? – was, oh she didn't know, but a kind of hospitality. Yes, that was right. It meant they still had a secret to offer, here in Venice. Something to reveal. And so goodbye. Would he cast off the painter, please?

Amedea had rowed away, who later that week would declare to Nancy Goncharov that she had no idea whether Gérard had hot water in that attic of his or not.

Back upstairs, Gérard regarded the black, malodorous heap of clothes on his bathroom floor. He fetched a rubbish bag, stuffed them into it.

By late March, Gérard Charry was getting about the city's waterways, though his sculling still lacked elegance. During April, he just about stopped chipping green paint off the gunwhales – although still, if the tide were against him, he found it hard to keep pace with the ricketiest crone creeping along a quay with her basket.

Amedea showed him how to thread his way through other craft. She devoted whole evenings to his cornering, trying to get him to turn the *s'ciopon* neatly where he wanted, not yaw all over the canal. Then she would inspect his hands, tell him his blisters were in the wrong places, he must still be holding his oar badly.

Gérard came to know Venice's original mesh of canals

as well as he knew the later mesh of streets imposed over it. Amedea taught him to avoid the canals around Campo Manin and Santa Maria Formosa, because it was dull to slouch along among the processions of tourist gondolas you kept getting log-jammed among there. She taught him to shelter under a bridge when a squall of rain came soughing down. (Why for me? wondered her pupil. And why these initiations into her Venetian arcana? Because she is too proud to commit adultery, every Jack and Jill do it, why should she? For naturally half Venice thinks we're having an affair. Because she is still in love with her husband? No, no, she can't be. But she is not unhappy in her marriage, either.) She taught him how to shorten his oar in shallow canals when the tide was low and scull with only a few inches of blade. (Because she hasn't got the guts to resolve never to see me again, Gérard hoped.) She taught him to scull along the narrowest ditches with the oar's handle slanted forward and the blade winnowing hard by the hull. (He was the second foreigner to whom she had imparted these mysteries. But each time he mulled over this fact it meant something different.) She taught him to shout a warning when he came to a blind turning – though his shout never sounded utterly Venetian in his own ears. Still, gondoliers didn't turn and stare. She taught him how not to let boats' wakes throw the *s'ciopon* off course. She taught him how to row crouching low on the floor-boards. That was useful, because then she could show him the dank rivulet that sucks and shivers in darkness beneath the floor of Santo Stefano. There weren't many people in the world who had sculled under the chancel of a church, she thought he might as well be of that company.

Gérard learned things about the mistress of the *s'ciopon* as well as how to manoeuvre it. She was thirty-one. She was the possessor of a Fortuny dress. It had belonged to her Lezze grandmother, and the next time there came a night when she might wear it – but they were getting pretty damned few and far between, life in Venice was horribly dull, she lamented – he must, he absolutely must, come and admire her. She had once swum the Grand Canal. Half drunk at Santa Maria del Giglio one night, Claudia Glaven and she had decided it was too far to walk round by the Accademia bridge; Claudia had shoved the key to Ca' Zante in her stockings or her knickers; they had dived in; they had swum; but when they had hauled themselves out on the palace jetty the key had gone, had sunk, and they shivered and sobered up a long time, Claudia's tawny mane sodden dark on her shoulders, because Ralph Chedgrave coming back on foot stopped at all the late bars.

Through the spring days, drifting in figures of eight about Venice from the Baia del Rè to the Garden of Eden, Gérard discovered that Amedea's hesitancy when she talked to him about Napoleonic barbarities, about sanctuaries, about having a secret to share, had been fake. An act, he was almost sure of it. An act to make her seem like other people . . . or to make him acknowledge some inner simplicity she thought she had and thought he would be moved by, was that it? Because natural to Amedea were directness, lucidity. "When I was a child and they discovered I could dance and sing, everyone said I should become an actress." She rolled her arrogance down the skittle alley of a conversation (this was into the hubbub of a table at Montin) with a master's amused eye on the slaughter of ninepins she'd wreak. "But I never wanted to be an actress. I've never wanted to be anyone but myself, not even for two hours each evening."

And yet, and yet, there were more and more things he wasn't discovering, things he didn't understand, Gérard would think peevishly, and hate himself for blushing alone in his attic as yet again he said to the telephone that he was free (free! his face would heat afresh miserably) and would like to come out in the boat, yes really, quite at liberty this morning, he would be on the quay in ten minutes' time. There was the Amedea Lezze who at babbly parties babbled; who on the beach cultivated her sun tan; who at the opera during the interval said what she thought of the singers. The most conventional, characterless of women, then? But how unreasonable to expect her to behave otherwise! There was the Amedea who with her husband was teasing and affectionate. ("He brings Heidegger to bed!" she had mourned giggling; but winking at Guy, Gérard had observed. "He lies beside me with his glasses on, reading Bergson! Claudia darling, what can I do?") The Amedea who with her blithe friends was blithe, with the sad sad. Who fussed over her child. Well, you couldn't expect her to have the Dead Sea scrolls laid up in her breast for the future to try to decipher, could you? Though something as idiotic as that was what Gérard was afraid he *was* coming to believe. As if somehow behind Amedea's always doing the obvious, simple, commonplace thing – behind her not being particularly imaginative about how she behaved – her just feeling and doing and saying what, for someone in her circumstances, came to hand . . . No, no! Gérard growled to himself, and grabbed a mooring post so she could step ashore, because she liked showing him her favourite churches and here they were at San Giacomo dell'Orio which as it happened he knew well but would be happy to visit again, horribly happy to visit with her. No! Nothing! But all the same . . . what was it? Not a Dead Sea scroll in her breast. Nothing to be deciphered. Nothing, perhaps, that could be written in any language. But as if hidden inside Amedea's ordinary this and trite that . . . (For her family and friends: affection, jokes. For society: social twitter, mild duplicities.) As if inside this were an enormous, simple hope – more hidden than a Dead Sea scroll, and abstract, abstract – a hope, once you had sensed it, utterly obvious – a faith utterly mad but which for any dull soul in banal circumstances might be the simple, ethereal thing that came to hand . . .

No! Gérard hung on to the mooring post. It was just longing for Amedea and not being able to have her because she was Guy's wife that made him dream up this crap.

They sculled on, not far, just to San Zan Degolà, which was shut. As it had been shut, Gérard said, when he had come once before, on foot, alone. But here was the Amedea Lezze who of course knew who had the key; who strode across the sunny, empty, grassy square; who knocked on a door; who was recognised with delight. And then when they came out of the little church and rowed away, when Gérard cleared his throat, cleared his throat again, and confessed that Francesca would have nothing to do with him any more, there was the Amedea who said quietly, seriously, how sorry she was. In fact, she said, she had suspected something might be amiss, because Francesca last night, clearly unhappy, had gone early to bed. And then there was the Amedea who slowly began to smile, and who slowly asked, "So . . . I wonder . . . What will you feel now?"

The day after his miracle, Gérard had telephoned the Lezze house to say thank you for the party and to ask Francesca Ziani if she would have dinner with him. No, she had said. Not Wednesday night. No night. Please, he was to try to understand. Oh yes of course one future night, and she would try to explain some time she promised, at dinner some far future night, and she would always be his friend, she knew that sounded laughable cliché but it was true, ah he was to believe her please. Gérard's first reaction had been relief. Then he had felt guilt because strolling homeward a few hours before he had contemplated marrying her – and now to feel relief that she wouldn't see him! But he didn't feel very guilty, because he at once started wondering what had caused Francesca's volte-face, and didn't take long to conclude she must have come to suspect Amedea and him (though how, he couldn't think – Francesca didn't have that sort of perceptiveness did she?) which, since it meant that very probably therefore he wasn't brainsick, there *was* something to suspect, conceivably a devastation in Amedea's heart the image of the devastation in his, made him dizzy with joy.

And now Amedea was rowing him out to the lagoon. He

could row competently with one oar, she told him, and two churches were enough for a while. Now she was going to teach him to row *ala valesana* with both oars. There were other things he must learn too. To row *a prua* in the bow while she rowed *a poppa* in the stern, or the other way round.

"It's a kind of dancing we can do together," Amedea said, looking him steadily in the eye, unblushing, mouth beginning to smile. (She never blushed. It was a skill Gérard suspected she would have liked to acquire, for use when she wished to seem innocent. Ah, why even at his most bewitched couldn't he stop mean thoughts?) And, "Oh!" she cried – for they were in open lagoon now, her lagoon where the egret fished – "doesn't it feel good that men and women have been sculling these boats on this water for hundreds of years, a thousand, more? This action and this place have proved good a long time," she declared firmly – but then suddenly seemed overtaken by confusion. "I mean . . ." she fumbled. "They're not likely to – well, I suppose what I . . . I hope they don't let us down now."

The lesson in rowing *ala valesana* commenced. But Gérard, in the effort to cross his oars, was still giving his knuckles fearful knocks when Amedea interrupted it. "Look," she said softly, and gestured with her eyes to where the breeze was blowing white and blue, the islands stood in new leaf, the reaches sparkled. "I've always . . . always come back here to . . . to get my courage back, get my faith in myself back. It's so even, I get an evenness in my head." She laughed. "Or the peace seems to lap in my head, or something. Does it lap in yours?"

That evening, they rowed to San Nicolò dei Mendicoli, where an old man kept monkeys in his garden. When the monkeys had been small and charming, they had been sold to credulous Venetian seamen in ports of Africa and India. On the voyages home, the monkeys had grown. This was contrary to what their previous owners had sworn. But some of the apes grew nearly as big as the sailors, who found them troublesome to feed and well-nigh impossible to control. Certainly they became unsuitable as presents for sweethearts at home. So a lot of animals were killed, till one old merchant skipper took pity on them.

He planted posts in his garden. He made a canopy of wire netting. As years passed and monkeys arrived and monkeys bred, he moved out of the ground floor of his house, removing the doors and windows to make life easier for his guests. By the time Amedea took Gérard to look at the church by the ruined cotton mill, and then to visit the monkeys across the *campiello*, the first floor had become a simian alms-house too. The monkeys made dejected noises in the rooms and trees they had fouled. Behind a pane of glass on the top floor, a withered human face looked down.

Disgusted by the monkeys, dejected by the old sailor, turning away, suddenly Gérard knew what he could offer Amedea as a gift equal to the oarsmanship and the lagoon she had offered him, equal to the boat a yard had undertaken to build for him, a boat which was her present to him, her supreme gesture – how could he doubt it? – despite the fact that he'd refused her offer to lend him the money.

His miracle. Why hadn't he thought of it before? So returning through the *campiello*, back round the church, back to where they'd tied up the *s'ciopon*, he told her how, walking home from her house that night, at an instant, miraculously, his head had been a sound-box where the ecstasy of transience reverberated. How since then, though his miracle hadn't come back – but it might, it might! – he had known himself to be living always in the beginnings of dissolution; how he liked that.

When he had finished, Amedea seemed thoughtful. She didn't say anything. Then lightly she kissed his cheek.

"Come to the Arsenale?" Francesca was bewildered. "It's military. I mean naval. They won't let us in there."

"Guy can get us in," her cousin declared. "I want Gérard to see the place."

Oh God I hadn't thought of that! Francesca wailed voicelessly. For it was true. The Arsenale was due to be ceded from naval to civil authority; Guy Ashmanhaugh was one of the architects who had been commissioned to draw up plans for its repair and adaptation; naturally he had a permit, came and went as he pleased. And she heard herself blurt out, "You can't make Guy do that!"

"Why not?" Amedea asked, and looked surprised.

Francesca Ziani, who when she had told Gérard she didn't want to see him any more had felt vile because she had allowed herself to dream (yes, yes, she made herself confront it squarely, bleakly, she had) of a love to crown all, all – well anyhow, the common garbage – had briskly stopped herself brooding on anything so inane. Had begun, instead, to feel guilty about Guy. For had he not, by telling her she was a what? a lure? a thing of rags, thread, feathers . . . Had he not gone further in the giving of himself up, in the loathsome making of himself defenceless, in his apparently studied offering of himself to any wayward insult and injury? Had he not left Amedea and Gérard to go – while he was in his studio with Mauro Zanier, while he was on site here or there, while he was at meetings with clients, lawyers, officials – rowing paradisally around Venice with nothing better to do than get obsessed with one another till the crack of doom, till the last high tide? And now it was June; and they were all to go to the Arsenale; and a divine and imbecile and fretful hand, Francesca thought, had been opening and shutting a chest of drawers, Guy Ashmanhaugh had been picked out of the drawer of ease like a sock and tossed into the drawer of pain; and what could anyone do about it?

Nothing. Nothing at all. They were to go to the Arsenale. Amedea commanded. So it would be. She wanted to show

Gérard Charry the dead heart of her city, the vital machine that had been less and less use, had been let break down, had been wrecked – while around it a few of the limbs of Venice still twitched. Twitched – no more than twitched. The population under ninety thousand and still dropping fast, for there were no jobs, only outsiders could afford a flat. The lagoon more polluted each year. People going out of business: drapers, ironmongers, grocers, everyone; because the only shops that made money were those that sold rubbish to tourists. But in the midst of all this public shame stood the Arsenale. And Amedea wanted to show it to Gérard. She would introduce him to the most secret place of all. (Ah Francesca could imagine it all too well! imagine it jealously, then with a big effort not jealously, then jealously again.) She would take him to the most private ruin. She would entertain him at the most exclusive though most dilapidated club in Europe to which only two caretakers and their wives, five dogs, twenty sailors, fifty cats and a thousand rats belonged.

The *s'ciopon* came in from the lagoon past collapsing walls, a coaster that had been being refitted for years, acres of derricks and brambles, one dry dock still in working order, a fuel dépôt. Then round into the Darsena Grande, that basin with no shipping now, a grey mirror picked out with the smeary colours of spilt oil and a few off-white blobs that were gulls.

All over Venice, people were doing things they often did. Franco Tagliapietra was in his studio, painting a sky. Etienne Maas was in his, drawing a girl. In a light aircraft high over the Lido, Ralph Chedgrave and Claudia Glaven and Comandante Paolo (who had been an enthusiastic fascist, whose brawny forearms always seemed about to burst the gold links of his gold watch, who wore a gold cross in the white mat on his chest, who liked boys) were levelling out; and Ralph was yelling, "Do it again Comandante, loop the bloody loop again would you, it keeps the snow up my nose in the most fucking wonderful way!" waving his silver cocaine spoon. While below them on the beach, young men and women lay farmed for their skins like crocodiles.

Drifting in the empty Darsena Grande amidst empty docks, empty boatyards, empty sail-makers' lofts, amidst roofless workshops and thickety yards, Guy discussed which buildings it might interest the newcomer to see. What about the Corderie, the pillared gallery over three hundred yards long where they used to make rope?

But it was Amedea, naturally, who decided where they should land. (Why did all Venice take her whims for commandments? her cousin wondered despondently. And oh why, *why* had she let herself be swept along on this expedition?) "The Gagiandre," Amedea said. So here they were now, tying up at the Gagiandre, which were docks, renaissance docks. Here they were, scrambling ashore. Grit and birdshit on marble. They dusted their knees, their hands. (She should never have come, Francesca berated herself, never! But Amedea had said, "Of course you're coming with us! It'll be fun." And now it would be a triumph if she contrived not to burst into senseless tears.) Shadow under the roof. Doric capitals. A mouldering picket-boat. Other warps that hung down and moored nothing.

Francesca heard Guy talking about possible reasons why the piers had been built at a slant from the wharf. She ought to concentrate, it would be interesting to find out. She watched him stand as he always stood, his right elbow cupped in his left hand, his right hand at his chin. Now he was pointing out the asymmetries of the roof, they were all craning their necks back.

And Gérard . . . Suddenly Francesca knew the Gagiandre were not the heart of whatever it was that this year was leading him like a bull led by a ring in its nose – for it was little better than that Francesca suspected, no, feared, no, knew, moving to stand a few paces apart. The Gagiandre were not the heart, though they stood so enigmatically in their hectares of ruins and creeks and silence.

Now Gérard was asking Guy when they were built. Guy was showing him the tablet with the five shields and the year 1573. (Francesca was obscurely convinced that date would wedge in her wits till she died.) Amedea was watching this going on. Amedea was the heart.

But she's fobbing him off, Francesca decided, relieved. (She would take an interest in the intricacies of the beams.) Yes, she's fobbing him off with oarsmanship, the Gagiandre, odds and ends, a boat being built. Like – but it was bitter! her mind flinched – she fobbed him off, perhaps, with me.

Or . . . Francesca flushed, she sidled further away through the weeds in the masonry. What if oarsmanship and the Gagiandre and a new boat and she her wretched self were the ways Amedea was leading Gérard after her while she – while she went – where?

Let her be cheating him, Francesca prayed.

Burano was the island for having boats built. As for which yard, Amedea took Gérard to Marco Zanon because his father Gasparo, who was still alive, had built craft for her father. Then there were half the vessels of the lagoon to choose from – which one did Gérard want?

Not a *San Pierotta*, though they are seaworthy and sail pleasantly, because Gérard wanted a boat light enough to row long distances alone. Not a *s'ciopon* because Amedea had one. Not a *mascareta*, although they are light and rakish and fast, nor a *puparin* with a raised stern-deck like a gondola, because the amateur oarsman was hardly equal to such sophistication, such grace.

So it was a *sandolo* the Zanon father and son built. An old design – they hadn't changed since the Renaissance,

Gérard discovered, looking at paintings. His boat would be steady enough, and have enough freeboard, to be dependable if a wind blew up when he was far from the city. The hull would be six or seven metres overall, and would cost a million lire.

This was about what was stored in the envelope that crumpled dustily on a beam in the attic along Fondamenta della Misericordia and was his frail defence against adversity. But then there would be oars and *forcole* to pay for too. Amedea had introduced him to the old oar-maker at Santa Fosca. He made beautiful *forcole* in cherry and walnut, the grain of the wood so dense and true they never split, the bights so smoothly ground and polished you scarcely knew you were rowing – but they cost sixty or seventy thousand each. So did the fine oars of ash inlaid with beech. Gérard had never given his poverty much thought, but debts embarrassed him. Still, he borrowed from his friends, fifty thousand here and there, he was too enthralled by Amedea not to. He was so enthralled (this he managed to realise only sluggishly, hardly focus on at all) that he didn't feel ashamed he hadn't innocently, straightforwardly accepted the money she offered to lend him.

The first time Gérard saw his *sandolo* she was a wood-pile under a lean-to shed. Amedea took a sheet of paper. It had Cantiere Zanon printed at the top, and a picture of a fishing boat. She leaned it on the flank of a tarred *peata* that was being patched; she wrote that Marco Zanon undertook to build for Gérard Charry a *sandolo* which . . . The whole thing took less than ten scrawled lines. They signed it. Then the party adjourned round the corner for *ombre* and octopus and bread and beans.

The second time, the boat was a roughly hewn skeleton. She had planking, strakes, a transom, ribs, but with inches of daylight at her seams. The mahogany for her gunwhales and decking and thwart stood propped against a saw-bench. So did the wood for her floor-boards.

They had gone in the evening – Guy, Corrado and Francesca too, Amedea had marshalled them so it was obvious she was just helping a friend have a boat built. By day there were only Signor Marco and Signor Gasparo, a tiny old man with bandy legs, a tobacco-leaf face, hands scarred by chisels that had slipped, finger-tips flattened by hammers that had missed. But in the evening other men came from other work; the two-litre bottle of Merlot was unstoppered. Then a vessel could take shape quickly. They built by eye.

"*Do something!*" Francesca had begged Guy; and had thought: Wake her out of her trance! "What about the yacht, what about *Zenobia*? There's one of your rituals that isn't getting performed this year. Why aren't Amedea and you getting her ship-shape for her summer cruise? Where was it you wanted to go this year, Sicily?" And he had muttered, "It's not that," or "It wouldn't do any good," or something. (For how could he inflict his middle-aged despondency on her innocence? How explain that if the old light and warmth Amedea and he had shared were failing, weren't much of a glory these days – if he was a faltering luminary, perhaps had never been a luminary at all – if she could even contemplate a second illumination – their marriage was no longer something he could desire?) Francesca had not given up. One day she had marched him down to the marina where the cutter lay. The varnish on her decks was cracked, peeling. In the cabin, the bedding and the old clothes were damp. Everything was covered in dust. Francesca with her lips pursed had written a list. So many tins of varnish. Then diesel, water, oil, gas. A new spinnaker halyard, the old one was frayed, didn't Guy remember? He had nodded, smiled, made himself talk a little. (Having this girl lodging in the house the year his marriage guttered was almost more than he could endure. How should he ever bring himself to try to explain to her that Amedea's soul and his soul were model clippers made by an old sailor and launched each in its bottle? How when they fell in love the divine hand had carefully pulled the last cords, how the toy masts and sails had risen impossibly in their glass domes. Mere lucent glass. But where else would you house a toy like the idea of the soul? And better, surely, than smashing the glass so you could touch the clipper, possess, fiddle with, break? How he had never felt anything like it before or since, that swaying up of masts, trembling of sails. The trouble was, though, had he been fooled, had only half his beloved's sails been hoisted? And his own – every last rag hoisted, truly?) So when Guy and Francesca went ashore from *Zenobia*, he was relieved to see the chandlery had just closed. Tomorrow, she insisted. But the next day he said he was busy. She never got him back to the yacht. And now she was standing in the Zanon boat-shed, and outside in the June dusk on a patch of tussocky grass women were harvesting the clothes borne by spindly props and sagging lines. A light rain started to pock the tide, came misting down on mud-flats, on marsh, on creeks. Francesca noticed Guy leave the jovial party around the *sandolo*, step out on to the slipway.

Guy might believe in letting his wife make up her mind unharried – would she turn back toward him? turn further away, face Gérard more squarely? go on dithering? – but he had been unable not to beg her not to separate him from his son. He had told Francesca this. Told it with an effort, gruffly. (The girl's intentions were so obviously good when she bullied him with her, "*Do something!*" with her, "What are you going to *do*?" Oh her heart was in the right place all right.) And Amedea had promised that she would never separate Guy and Corrado. Never. Whatever happened. She had promised that, apparently, Francesca recalled, watching her raise her glass of wine, hearing her say, "To the *sandolo*!" And had added that she had told her lawyer to have the Miracoli house transferred into Guy's name. And Guy had been able to say nothing; he had stumbled out to the street – it had been after midnight, the *sestiere* ghostly – and as far as Verrochio's statue. There his mounted hero rode against the stars, paradigm of bitterness triumphant and of the sweetness of pride, auditor of gentlemen's spiritual accounts . . . that was how he thought of him anyway, Guy had confessed with sudden roughness – and Francesca could at least see, couldn't she, that it was difficult to conceive of Colleoni being betrayed by a woman, or caring if he were? Impossible to conceive of that. But he that night had been so relieved that it had felt like contentment. She would not take Corrado from him. Before the bronze horse and bronze rider, he had stood in thanksgiving. What did it matter if her giving him the house meant she was freeing herself, if it was sad for Corrado to have a mother who preferred freedom to him? Perhaps in fact it was not all that sad for Corrado. No. And then Guy had remembered that Amedea had broken her word before. Had she not sworn to love him always, to love only him?

Francesca had puzzled over this, tagging along with Amedea to parties. For although of Europe's ancient, glorious capitals Venice was now the smallest, the least powerful; muddy, sleepy; as cosmopolitan as ever but futilely so; provincial, but with her own people draining away; still that summer what tawdry nocturnal jamborees the Bride of the Sea still could stage witnessed that Amedea Lezze went to as many parties as ever, though almost never with her husband.

Francesca would still be tagging along at dawn when they returned to the Miracoli, went into the kitchen and made coffee, came out to the garden bench with their cups, kicked off their shoes, listened to the birds begin fifing in the greenery. Are these innocent delights or aren't they? she would wonder. For in a while Signora Donatella would come out of the house and stump wheezily to mass where she would pray, Francesca knew, for the marriage of the elegant, half drunk, but still technically chaste lady now scuffling her toes in a dusty flower-bed that smelled of cats' piss, telling silly stories about the people at dinner. But the summer nights were so short, how could they be grave indulgences? Short, sultry . . . Who was the Latin author, Francesca couldn't remember, who in weather like that once failed to lift his languid hand, decided he'd have to change into his light, summer rings? Anyhow that was what it felt like. But then just before sunrise the air was fresh. She sipped her coffee, tickled Corrado's black kitten Strassa. Amedea was abstaining from her love affair, wasn't she? What harm was there in wriggling your toes in the dust and listening to the dawn chorus? Francesca would wriggle her toes too.

Then upstairs in what had been one of the Lezze maids' rooms she would unbutton her silk shirt – most of her clothes were presents from her rich cousin. She would lie down to sleep, while high over the roofs the first swifts of the day hawked after the first gnats.

But it would not be possible to sleep. There was no limit to people's mean-spiritedness – at radiant dawns, Francesca seemed to know it with weary decisiveness. For Guy was being criticised pretty widely in Venice, she had heard, criticised for his stillness and silence, the apparent indifference with which he let work on his marriage stop. Yes, like the Tower of Babel, she thought – that image had stayed with her, maybe because he was an architect. It was like that, the way Guy had let his marriage become a ruin from one month to the next. Francesca supposed that at the end the master-builder and a local potentate who'd dumped a lot of money in the project stood together on the highest ramp where work had been abandoned. Perhaps they did, perhaps they'd been friends, and gazed down past the soaring jackdaws and out through the soughing void and away to the low brown hills, and knew there'd be nothing to bind them together any more. No – with the fatigue of that sun burning on stone and scaffolding she expected they sat down, looked at the first weeds fluttering in cracks in the masonry. Was that what it was like for Guy and Amedea? And then still without speaking did they walk to where they'd left their horses a storey below on the shady side, mount and ride slowly, stirrup to stirrup, down ramp after ramp where no one would ever climb up again? Sleepily, Francesca would reckon it might be a bit like that. And something to do with them both being survivors of empires, maybe . . . (Guy had a perfect Raj voice, his wife would exclaim, an Empire voice, couldn't Francesca hear it? And of course she couldn't hear it.) Yes, she didn't think either of them found anything strange in the abandonment of half-built towers.

Now Francesca went to the boat-shed door. Where was Guy? Ah, there. He was standing alone at the foot of the slipway. No doubt he hadn't been able to stand the brightness in his wife's eyes when she had rapped her fingers on the *sandolo*, had asked Gérard, "Well? Are you pleased? Don't you think Signor Marco is brilliant?"

Francesca walked toward Guy. A puddle had collected on the tarpaulin over a *batela* on a cradle; it overflowed, dripping on the skids. She reached him, put her hand through his elbow. The rain fell harder, drilled the pale bergs of froth drifting by in the gloaming, began to flatten them and break them up.

From the shed doorway Corrado yelled, "Papa! *Vien' qua!*"

Guy turned, said, "I must try harder to make him speak English sometimes."

The third time Gérard Charry saw his *sandolo* she was ready to launch, painted blue and grey from the ironwork on her prow to that on her stern. She lay on trestles on the slipway in the July morning sun.

Every man who had lent a hand building the boat was there to launch her. (It was the day of the Festa del Redentore, no one had gone to work.) Gérard bowed his ignorant head among the knowledgeable heads bowed over the starboard gunwhale to fit one *forcola*, then over the port gunwhale to fit the other. Voices piled up higgledy-piggledy in his ears, he couldn't disentangle them. The second *forcola* didn't fit, a chisel was fetched, decisions were taken, a plane was fetched.

Often he doubted that Amedea was in love with him. But not that morning, with the *sandolo*'s hull painted so freshly, mahogany top-sides varnished so shiningly. And when Francesca had confronted him point-blank, he had replied: Yes, I am in love with Amedea. I don't know what's going to happen. Nothing, probably. Sometimes I hardly think it matters if nothing happens; maybe possessiveness is not one of my vices; but I am in love with her, yes. And Francesca had retorted – no, not retorted, she had besought, knitting her plump fingers: If it doesn't matter what happens, leave Amedea's marriage alone! leave Guy and Corrado be! And he had answered: I am leaving Amedea alone. There was Francesca now, with her little second cousin in her arms, watching the *forcola* being planed. No doubt she was piously hoping the *sandolo* was the limit of what he would be given; hoping Amedea would turn him loose now on the lagoon as a horse is turned loose in a pasture; hoping he wouldn't be too sad.

A dear girl, Francesca. A dear sweet girl of course. But you couldn't expect her to understand how exhilarating was the balance between Amedea's stillness and silence in one pan of the scales and his in the other; how level the beam trembled; how airily poised she and he were. And he had tried to explain his miracle to Francesca, and it had been a dismal failure. But in May his mind had been fireworking so effulgently with the miraculous (there would be fireworks tonight for the Festa, he remembered, that would be fun) that when she had cheered up, had agreed to dine with him, he had told her everything. But it had been hopeless. That mutability was the very excitement of life itself – that transience gave the blessing of freedom – no, she hadn't understood at all.

"I'm sorry, I haven't given it a thought," Gérard said. And Marco Zanon, who had asked him what name the new boat was to be given, who had never launched an unchristened vessel before and was perplexed – was Gérard a Protestant? didn't they christen their boats? – turned to Guy and Amedea. Did the young man not have a girlfriend? Surely he must have. Then what was wrong with accustomed ways, could the *sandolo* not be given her name? But Amedea laughed. "Girls, Signor Marco? Gérard has so many, he'd have to rename his boat repeatedly. Scarcely worth beginning such a weary process, I'd say."

Well, now with any luck we can get the boat into the water, Gérard thought – for the troublesome *forcola* at last fitted snugly. If baptism could be skipped, soon he would be away – he shaded his eyes with his hand – toward those wooded islands. He'd been wrong about Francesca. She hadn't got much feeling for this – this – what was it? That a marriage, he vaguely supposed, in order to be such, must needs be this and be that – but a love affair could be anything, could be nothing, couldn't it? Might take any of the infinite forms of life. Might be abstract. Might be, for example, the perfect balance between two stillnesses, two silences. ("Lift!" he said in chorus with Marco Zanon, for his *sandolo* was coming off the trestles at last, at last!) It might be made up, of course, largely, as one made up the best part of life. But an exquisite amusement.

And what did it matter if he could hardly believe in this perfect balance, Gérard thought, hearing the splash as the hull hit the water. For who was he?

One so unworldly that he never had more than ten thousand francs in hand, often not five thousand, and today, having just paid Signor Marco, was in debt. One so dreamy that quite a small, weak miracle had bowled him over first swipe. (But Amedea had understood that joy of his. She had accepted the gift of his miracle, he knew, because in answer she had told him about the evenness of lagoon-light, how it played in her mind; she had asked, Did it play in his mind, that peace? had wanted to give it to him.) One whose ceiling leaked in storms, so he had to get out of bed in the middle of the night to set buckets and saucepans under the drips. (So he had guessed right! Gérard rejoiced. Hidden in the wife and mother, hidden in the society flutterer, was the enormous, simple hope of one water-light that might dazzle two minds' eyes as one.) But he! A sitter on bridge parapets at night. A watcher for the goddess of daybreak who, wearing a bathing dress, would come water-skiing ashore at whichever church she had chosen that morning, kick off her skis and, as if it were the most normal thing in the world, just our way of entering our temples in the West, lean them against the church door, go inside.

Still Gérard Charry was not allowed to get aboard his *sandolo* and row away. It seemed every man on the slipway had to scull the new boat up the channel and back, had to agree she was built light, built strong, had to express a judgement on oars and *forcole*.

Then at length his craft was handed over to him – but only provisionally, because no one on the landing stage believed very profoundly that he could row, not being from the lagoon. But Amedea's second pupil didn't disgrace her. (Her first stood watching, his right elbow in his left palm, the fingers of his right hand stroking his chin.) He was awkward, but away he went under the eyes of the sages. Guy and Amedea, Francesca and Corrado, followed in the *s'ciopon*.

But what could it matter, Gérard demanded of the island

of San Francesco del Deserto as he rowed past its monastery, cypress grove, wharf, if he would never be able to buy his attic with its roof cats and its view of the Servi garden and its winter leaks? Or even if next year the university decided to economise by not renewing his contract, or decided to give his post to some professor's protégé, and he had to give French lessons to pay the rent – he'd done that before, in bad years – would that matter much? Or that he was so given to distractedness that at an exhibition standing before a painting he would sometimes fall into such a reverie, go practically to sleep on his feet like the mules he had seen carrying logs in the Appenines when they were let stop and rest, that when he remembered himself with a start, his mind ringing with clarion dreams whose echoes died away swiftly, he couldn't ever retain much.

These things didn't matter, because a monk chugging along in a barge raised his hand courteously. Because they had decided to row homeward down the winding Sant'Erasmo channel, and the island lay green on the blue. Because in the shoals a fisherman had planted his oar and had tethered his skiff to it, now he was wading nearby, stooping, peering into the shallows, straightening.

Naturally, if Amedea ever decided she wanted a separation – and why should she be left to get stale in a dim, chilly marriage like a piece of meat splatted down on a plate, left in a larder? – it would be important to be enormously nice to Guy. Who was a splendid fellow. They'd only met half-a-dozen times, but Gérard had no doubt about that. Guy was affable when you talked to him, though his face in moments of solitude could look morose. Odd – he didn't seem to love his wife very gaily or passionately. And it can hardly be her teaching me to row, Gérard thought, which has made him so gloomy, dug those ditches from his nose to his mouth. Because I've never telephoned their house; never written her a letter; never asked her to dinner; nothing. And of course it would be important also to make sure Corrado spent lots of time with both parents . . . But all that kind of thing went without saying – Gérard was blithe, sculling past Ca' La Vela – didn't it? Why did people whine so righteously about marriages coming to grief? People, he thought, were rather easily dismayed. Anyhow, it was unlikely Amedea would ever be his lover, let alone wish to scrap her husband for his sake. (But it was getting to be almost more than he could endure, kissing her calmly, lightly on both cheeks when they met, the way they both kissed all their friends.) And now, right now, more important by far than all these things was that towering cloud slowly drifting across the blue wash sky, high white rampart heaped on white rampart, southern breastwork tinged with gold. Jerusalems, Gérard called them. He didn't know why. A phrase picked up from his father maybe. (His mother wrote that she had changed her diet, had discovered Jesus, had a new psychotherapist.) And certainly the City of God would look like that if it existed, would parade its battlements that majestically across the sky, sail out of sight that quietly.

And if Amedea never came to him . . . Still she would have given him those nightfalls when they lit the lantern – one evening the new moon had been cuddling the old – and stayed out in the *s'ciopon* while dew glistened on the planks, winding in the labyrinth of the city's canals. And that time in broad day when he'd been dawdling at his oar along Rio della Maddalena and there was a swarm of bees seething on a house wall, people were chucking open their windows and calling across the canal, banging their windows shut when the uproarious swag looked like coming loose. Or the day they sculled under Ponte Tre Archi and there was scaffolding up. "Yesterday I had lunch with Gloria," Amedea had been saying. "She talks with her mouth full. Why doesn't Carlo ditch her?" But then she had looked at the bridge and said, "All three arches," and smiled. "Body, mind, spirit." Her smile had become a laugh. "They're going to be restored. Aren't we lucky?"

So gliding forward at sea-level in his new *sandolo* that

summer morning with the towers and domes of Venice way ahead, Gérard knew he was standing on the highest pinnacle of his luck. All the lagoon was his, he'd hardly begun his possession yet. And Amedea had given it him, all that blocked sea mouldering in its black pit . . .

He could even have it without her – what else did his boat mean? – so magnificently she gave.

Guy rowed the *s'ciopon* except when Francesca asked if she could have a turn; but she gave the oar back after a quarter of an hour. He helped Corrado tow *Hispaniola* astern. *Hispaniola* had been bought at Hamley's last time he was in London; she was nearly two foot, had a bowsprit, blue sails; had her grand name because he was telling the child simple bits of *Treasure Island* at bed-time, preparatory to their reading it in a couple of years.

A light breeze got up. Guy stepped the mast, hoisted the gaff and the patched tan sail. He sat on the floor-boards, leaned his back against the gunwhale, steered by trailing an oar angled against the *forcola*. A hundred yards off, there was hopeless Gérard pushing at his oar. No, not hopeless, but Guy suspected he was pretty ineffectual – he'd never finished his thesis, was that right? And it seemed he spent half his mornings sleeping off his nights' dissipations. And he had had that interminable, futile so-called love affair with Cecilia Zancana, who should have had more sense – anyway he was besotted with Amedea these days. Now he had picked up his second oar (the *sandolo* hadn't been rigged with a mast and sail) and was rowing *ala valesana* or trying to, pretty ungainly, wobbling like hell when a ferry's wake swelled.

Calm, calm, Guy Ashmanhaugh ordered himself. It's

happened to better men than you, this business (well-chosen, off-hand word) of having a good-looking young fool fall in love with your wife, and she half – half? – in love with him. Do not think of it as nightmarish; think of it as irritating.

Guy looked at Amedea where she lay on her back on the floor-boards; head pillowed on a book; dark glasses warming in the blazing air (her eyes must be shut, but he couldn't see them); her bikini top lying crumpled beside her. This Italian woman's zeal for goldenness, Guy thought, who hadn't taken off his ruined calico hat with a green silk puggree that remained from Nilgiri Hills days, let alone his trousers and shirt. Why could he no longer desire her in the present, only in the past? his heart grieved with such sudden vehemence that tears prickled as if they'd been sparkling mineral water. For it was impossible to be calm, out of the question to be merely and wisely irritated, when he knew it was his inability to long for his wife now, his inability to believe there was anything one could substantially do to combat ethereal feelings, that were turning him to a statue, to a stone figure of cold grief, a mossy Despair at the gate to a vault, whom Amedea would find it hard to go on loving very vibrantly or very long.

Ethereal feelings! Bullshit. It was lust. Amedea's longing to lay hands on Gérard felt like an anvil in Guy's chest, a dead weight he couldn't lift out of his heart, put down, walk away from. And the idea of Gérard laying hands on her, of her excitement, was an anvil in his head.

She lay beside him. The sort of canvas that would sell for a fat sum, he thought. *Woman Sunbathing in a Boat* – something like that. Of course, when you didn't make love with your wife any more it was all over. Why couldn't he want to? Why couldn't he lift the anvil out of his chest, lift the other anvil out of his head, take Amedea off to the hills for a week, to Asolo for instance, they'd had idylls in Asolo in the past, and walk through the hills and meadows and come back for dinner and make love? Fastidious – squeamish . . . Throat never quivering; mouth never dry. No feelings, his sombre face showed these days. No feelings showed through his temperate conversations. He leaned on the gunwhale; he steered by angling his oar.

And ah why when Guy looked at Amedea was he tormented with nothing more useful than the desire for this spring and this summer never to have been? (A fly settled on her breast. Her hand brushed it away. He saw Gérard's hand, saw her smile.) For what Guy ached for was a lost Amedea loving and true who on board the *s'ciopon* at Sant'Erasmo regatta had lifted her glass of wine; had seemed to drink not only to him but to the island trees and the racing skiffs and the tideway too; had seemed to believe their marriage a component part of the scene, laughing and declaring as she declared every year that next year she was going to recruit a gargantuan fellow oarswoman and win the ladies' race, what about that roundabout puce-countenanced baggage over there, wielding her oar like a rolling pin? Though now as Guy gazed at her it came to him that her head could take any quantity of light. Rays were falling on her lips, her cheeks, her brow, her bobbed black hair. He imagined shafts of heat and brilliance lancing through skin, muscle, blood, bone. Her opaque mind was laid there, offered to these converging brightnesses. Behind those black lenses, behind those translucent eyelids, those grey eyes – were they truly shut? – her greymatter must be flushing pink and gold.

Stop it! Stop it, you fool! Guy yanked his gaze away.

There lay Sant'Erasmo where smallholders kept rabbits and bantams in a ruined tower, bred fish in the pools. Where in winter the tracks were hard with frost, rime whitened the sedge and bull-rushes, cat-ice floated on the ditches. Where the alders lifted a bare ruche of twigs against brown December clouds. Where teal winnowed the cold with their fast wing-beat, brack slid past the quays.

What was all this yearning for winter for? Just that Amedea hadn't met Gérard till Lent? The first sign of spring on the island was good too: a haze of purple in the alder clumps. When warm days came, the islanders netted their fig trees and plum trees to keep the birds from the ripening fruit. At midday they ate under arbours in cottage yards, Guy and Amedea strolling past had envied them. Frogs croaked in the swamps and ponds, plopped into the water if you came too near.

Guy had so often been happy on Sant'Erasmo with Amedea, he was sure that if he went there alone now he was wretched it would have a good effect if he didn't exploit it too often. He would walk through the orchards, put up egret from the fish-ponds. Perhaps he would see a heron or a bee-eater. At evening farmers would water their small-holdings. Boys and girls would stroll in the village square. He could lean on the sea-wall with the old men with cigarettes and the young women with babies, watch the fishing-boats. He could go to the one *bacaro* on the island where there was nothing to drink but sour Raboso, nothing ever to do but contemplate the damp patches on the walls and listen to the men play dominoes. Peace might come, or renunciation or . . . He could wander back into the fields, lie on a dyke, watch the twilight go violet and the moon come up.

No. Sant'Erasmo was too near. Guy wanted to go to India, go home.

Captain Ashmanhaugh had survived the fall of Malaya to the Japanese. He had survived prison and the death of friends. In 1945 his wife had found him three parts dead. She had taken him back to India, to his tea plantation. She had nursed him there. Captain Ashmanhaugh had lived long enough to see the crop returned to nineteen thirties productivity; to teach Viola the essentials of tea farming; to see his son Guy born in a shuttered bedroom of the wooden bungalow while a punkah flapped. Then he had died.

He had left Guy his MC, his cups won steeplechasing and playing polo. A Lee Enfield, a Mannlicher, three shot-guns.

Lances for tent-pegging. Some Indian harness and saddlery.

The big tea company had complied with Mrs Ashmanhaugh's eccentric request to continue to manage the plantation. The commercial future of the newly independent nation was obscure. Even more cloudy were the reasons the young widow might have for not wishing to return to England to, presumably, marry again. But the estate was prosperous, so for a while . . .

Viola Ashmanhaugh was still in the Nilgiris. And on the Venetian lagoon her son – really this desolation of his was shameful! he cursed himself, and probably better called self-pity – was grabbed by the scruff of his neck by the need to walk through Indian tea fields, as a terrier snatches a rat by the scruff, shakes it till its neck snaps. To walk in soft rain between shining hedges of tea. (But Amedea had visited the Nilgiri Hills with him; her spirit would be there; he must remember that, when the train stopped at Mysore and Corrado and he got out with their suitcases – for it was high time his mother saw her grandson again.) To watch a hawk veer over the hillside. To splash through mud. He might cheer up gradually, walking through tea bushes in warm monsoon.

Then Guy's skull was like *Zenobia*'s bilges: that grey, that cold. Despair was the shallow water that slopped to and fro and he couldn't pump out. Manfully he tried to be temperate. He was a temperate man, wasn't he? Indeed, wasn't it because he was a temperate man that he was losing his wife's love? Still, he thought, if you have a strength, even if it isn't the starriest of virtues, you'll fall all to pieces if you let that one thing go. So he wrestled, immobile and quiet at his steering-oar.

It was no good, he couldn't make the bilge pump work. (And the Lezze family lawyer had done as he had been bidden; the house at the Miracoli was Guy's now; he had received it as the final proof of his failure in love.)

He tried holding his mind very firmly: then at least the

grey water was still. Dimly in the murky bilge he could see the twists of tow hang still, the spots of oil float unbroken. Guy watched. The dropped shackle-pins, washers, screws sank and lay still. But when his mind quivered, when however hard he tried to hold it firm it swayed, the despair slopped about and he couldn't see anything.

The day was hot and still. The islands lay at anchor very stilly. Didn't I swear I'd be true to my miracle? Gérard cursed himself, clenching his sore palms on his oar. No whingeing after perpetuity, didn't I swear I'd remember? The trick is to renounce gracefully.

Amedea Lezze's mother had jiggled her life along conferring with priests. Her father, as upright a man as her father-in-law who had distinguished himself fighting the emperor Hirohito's fascists, had refused to have any truck with the dictator Mussolini's, and was in the Bologna printing workshop of a liberal news-sheet when he was arrested.

Michele Lezze's years in prison were unpleasant, but they bore no resemblance to the tortures Captain Ashmanhaugh endured on the Burma Railway. After the liberation, two months at home in the house at the Miracoli restored his health. The righteousness and blood-letting of 1945 revolted him, so he joined the diplomatic service to get abroad – an educated man, who had stood up to the tyrant and his flunkeys, could take his pick of the professions that year. In the new, democratic Italy, with relief and even with pride he gave up using his title, though he could not prevail upon his wife to stop people calling her *contessa*. He had four friends with peerages of varying antiquity and authenticity, all of whom went on being *barone* or *conte*. Three of them called him a ridiculous prig. The fourth accused him of having evolved a particularly nasty form of arrogance.

By the time his daughter Amedea was a schoolgirl, Lezze had given up his career. It was not, he would explain to friends, that he would not have liked to see if he could reach ambassadorial rank; but that the Christian Democrats, whom he had joined after the war and who had helped advance his career, had revealed themselves such pious, hypocritical, venal parasites that he preferred to dissociate himself. (To his wife, after he had despondently contemplated a dozen feeble-sounding reasons why she would never be the first lady at an ambassadorial ball, he announced that sheer, laughable, old-fashioned patriotism – why should a Venetian serve a Roman government? – mixed with nostalgia for his boyhood, had convinced him their child should be brought up on the lagoon.) And to that daughter he confessed a year or two before his death, when she was seventeen and unruly, he white-headed at fifty, and they used to drift around Venice together in the *s'ciopon* on sunny evenings, that of recent years he had taken to voting communist. Not that he could take the Dictatorship of the Proletariat any more seriously than the Redemption of Sins, but . . . "Well, my dear, I'm afraid they're the only honourable bunch in our unlucky country's public life." And she in her turn would confess. No, she was not a virgin; yes, she quite liked hashish. He would not criticise her. He would tug his moustaches. He would not lay down the law – he who with all his advantages had never come to much, had never governed, hadn't even written a travel book or a biography, hadn't even sailed for his country in the Olympic Games though he'd come near it once. The only interesting thing he had done for years had been to fly his own aeroplane. When on a foggy day in the Dolomites it hit a mountain, there was one goodbye he might have had to try not to smile at. In the garden of his old friend Nancy Goncharov's palace one night, his daughter remarked to her hostess, "I'm damned glad he had his wife with him when he crashed. She hated flying. It's almost as if he knew . . ." Shrugging; smiling at her own bitchery. "As if he were thinking of me when he took her up that day."

Now Amedea Lezze lay in the *s'ciopon* being rowed home to Venice by her husband – for the wind had died to nothing, he had unstepped the mast. She liked the hard floorboards where she lay; liked the hard sun – it was near its zenith now – beating on her. Behind her dark glasses she opened her eyes in time to see Guy sway forward steadily with the stroke of his oar; in time to see him look down at her where she lay; see that at the sight of her all the knots in his cat's-cradle heart pulled tight, see his mouth twitch as he realised he'd never untie them.

Amedea waited a couple of heart-beats till Guy had finished his swing forward, till he swayed back upright. Then she propped herself on one elbow. Instantly Guy's face was controlled. His voice was kind. "Are you hot? There's some water in that bottle."

Amedea screwed her head around, saw Francesca and Corrado curled up sleepily in the bow. The *s'ciopon* and the *sandolo* were idling along in convoy past the island of Le Vignole: woods, marsh, a house or two. Venice lay full in view – an intricate, luminous work of jewellery it looked, Amedea thought. A tiny city made of sapphires, of rubies, of amethysts, of emeralds, encrusting a turquoise sea. Turquoise sea, really? Well, with that sun-dazzle she couldn't see the scum, the froth, the dead weed, the poisoned fish, the sullage. And there lay Murano with its lighthouse, and San Michele the graveyard island, and . . . She turned, looked astern. Yes, Mazzorbo far away. How evenly the levels of light lay on the lagoon! It was so calm, she could almost sense the ideas and feelings in the air – was she mad? she was sure she was not – almost sense the desires drifting by on their inconclusive ways. And there was the good slowness of colours altering all day. Was the peace lapping in Gérard's head too? It must be! This, this, she had wanted to give him, had schemed that he should have. But how could she tell? There he rowed. He must be tired. But even if he had been beside her, if he had been close enough to touch, to kiss, she wouldn't have been able to tell if there were a feeling in his head akin to the feeling in hers. Trembling, trembling with the effort not to tremble, Amedea gazed. But how could she sense, by staring at his head – it was distant, it was small, it was round; it had no features; it swayed fore and aft as he rowed, fore and aft, fore and aft – how could she sense if the brilliance she loved were rippling there too? It was only a feeling – whatever a feeling was . . . But . . . As if by grace the same blood could suffuse two grey minds with one flush of rose.

Shivering in the heat, Amedea lay back on the hard, warm floor-boards. She must lie tranquil, lulled. Or offer to row instead of Guy; or row *a prua* while he rowed *a poppa*. But no. She didn't want to. And he would be least discontented with something to do, do alone; his womenfolk apparently somnolent; his child quiet and still.

But the creak of the oar didn't lull her. The sun's flamy licking of her arms and legs, her stomach and breasts and face (dry, warm kisses she thought, kisses of a dry, excited mouth) didn't lull her. The chuckle of ripples along the planks around her head didn't lull her as they had used to do, year after year of lazy days. Because she didn't know what to say, she must be silent. Because she didn't know what to do, she must be still. But it was anguish! It was impossible! She could feel her blood fizzing in her hands, even when she carefully kept all ten finger-tips on the floor-boards she was sure they were pitter-pattering. And the muscles of her thighs and stomach and throat were flickering, she was sure they were, Guy would only have to glance down as no doubt he was doing now and then, he'd see her skin drubbed from within.

And no one was any help. Claudia Glaven, after making a few cheerful enquiries, back in the spring, as to how her friend's amour was getting on, had quit asking, discouraged by the vague answers meted out. (Claudia had once passed a few hours in bed with Gérard Charry, and found Amedea's grand passion hard to take seriously.) Francesca didn't seem to disapprove quite so confidently; no longer judged her, Amedea felt, with quite such disgusting omniscience – doubtless she was getting over her jealousy; but these days she never breathed a word; she waited in girlish awe – Amedea was dismissive – for whatever fate the household at the Miracoli should be consigned to. Old Donatella disapproved of her love of course. But there was nothing she could do about it except pray, Amedea thought, and below her dark glasses gave a thin-lipped smile. Nothing Donatella could do except pray. Oh and make an irritating show of how, every time Gérard came and they put forth in the boat, she had to find some ploy for Corrado whose mother was frivolously . . . And he poor little darling knew nothing, never said a . . .

Rocked in the cradle of the *s'ciopon* (a barge had chugged by, its wake heaved) Amedea Lezze writhed. Then quickly, in confusion, she wacked at her flank. "Mosquito?" Guy asked. "No. Don't think so. Goddamned horse-fly, it felt like."

No, not a cradle, she thought, flat on her back again. It was an open coffin; Guy was Charon; he was rowing her to the graveyard island. Hidden by her black lenses, Amedea opened her eyes. There were his shoulders and his head, dark against the azure sky. He ought to have been a dashing young lieutenant in the Bengal Lancers fifty or a hundred years ago, and then a Sanskrit scholar, and then posted to Kabul – all that. Not an architect and her husband and Charon. It was obvious, with that British India voice of his, and the way he took Nietzsche on picnics, and held doors open for you.

Amedea's thoughts were skittering, she knew, but she couldn't stop them. Someone – she herself? – was playing ducks and drakes with the flat stones which were her thoughts, wouldn't stop skimming them away over the flat lagoon – and there a fish jumped, so they weren't all dead – till here, there and everywhere they stonily slowed, stonily would fly no further, stonily sank. She would try to think one thing, one! That Guy's Empire (British) voice had gone well with her Empire (French) table and four chairs left from shameful times when the house had been a billet for Austrian officers. It had seemed to go well too with her Empire (Venetian) love for a civilisation in decline, no, after its decline, nothing but memory. But then she might equally well think how when she first met Guy he had only just set up the practice with Mauro Zanier; how inspiring it had been, his determination to give his professional life to shoring up the ruins of La Serenissima – this wall, that roof. Or then again she could think how after her marriage she had gone on feeling islanded. She had hoped she would not; but she had. To stand alone sometimes in the *salone* of her house on quiet, soft afternoons, and to feel islanded. That was what the years had been like. To stand at twenty, then at twenty-five, at thirty. To gaze into the same glitter of canal-light sifting through flawed panes in the arches; to gaze at faded red and blue and yellow silk walls, wretchedly liver-spotted now, worn right through in places; at stabs of tarnished brilliance from cornice and chandelier, marble floor and picture frames. Venice was moated by the lagoon. She was half moated in her house. Islanded. Even after Corrado was born. Islanded – and he too . . .

And now she was lying in an open coffin, getting browner she supposed, and Charon was rowing her to the island of the dead. "Are we getting toward San Michele?" she asked. Yes, Guy said, they were quite close now. Another five minutes or so, and they'd be passing it. Perhaps she ought to put her shirt on, he suggested. There were boats about.

God, Amedea thought, clothes. To sit up, to blunder her arms into her shirt, because there were boats about. It was exhausting, when you were sheer cliché. For she was nothing but an assemblage of clichés – that struck her pretty forcibly now, landed with a rumbling crash on the paving of her mind like a lorry-load of rubble tipped out on to a roadside, landed with thudding and dust. Yes, she was rank cliché, the silly woman who had emerged horribly in love (but, she made herself snarl, it was probably only boredom and desire) and immobilised by indecisiveness in her thirty-second year amidst everyone else's considerately muffled concern, and who had now buttoned her shirt askew – honestly this was to play the scatter-brained sybarite too naturally – so she was having to unbutton it, start again. One cliché after another. Her family; wealth; looks – that bow mouth; junketings; marriage; son – the sweetheart! dissatisfactions; all derivative, it had all been done, thought, felt before. And now she would have a love affair. As Amedea realised this, she started to laugh. Yes – because that was what you did, when you were cliché through and through, didn't you? You had, under these circumstances, a love affair. She laughed and laughed. She wanted to yell across the water to Gérard that from sheer lack of originality she would be his. She wanted to tell Guy, share the joke. No she didn't.

Amedea shook, she chortled. In alarm, because it was not a pleasant laughter, Francesca asked, "What's funny?" But Amedea didn't tell her, and Guy wouldn't catch her eye.

Everyone was the soul of honour except her, Amedea knew that. After one of her solitary frettings about the city – she had been doing rather a lot of that, lately – she had fetched up at Franco Tagliapietro's studio. She had stopped him working, let him give her a glass of wine. She was in love with Gérard, she had announced to the room hung with skies, stacked with skies, to the sky on the easel, the sky outside the window. Franco had wiped his hands on a rag. He had plonked brushes into a jar. It would be a shame if a shadow were cast on Corrado's childhood, he had said. And of course, she knew, she would understand, Guy was an old friend of his. But she must make up her own mind.

Anthony Holt was the soul of honour too – as indeed you would expect in a man who knotted his bow-ties so elegantly. Amedea had not dared ask him what he thought. Poor Anthony, he was a friend of Gérard's as well as Guy's! And about as likely to pry or to bully as to go in for politics, or buy a television, or renounce his faith, or try to introduce any order into his ruinous house wedged with wardrobes full of theatrical costumes, stopped from falling down by the crammed bookcases from floors to ceilings, bulging to its paintless shutters and dead window flowers with piles of newspapers and magazines, with lame furniture, with dusty ornaments, with mysterious trunks, festooned with cock-eyed paintings and cobwebs, ringing with Brahms. Anthony was Corrado's godfather. He had conceivably been alluding to that when in May he had gone to Guy's studio one evening, they had come together back to the Miracoli, because Anthony had a pair of ebony hair brushes for the boy's birthday, which was not till November.

Was Nancy Goncharov the soul of honour, or had she just been amusing herself? In the *s'ciopon*, Corrado had woken up; his mother, decently shirted, knelt beside him on the floor-boards, helped him couple a blue tractor to a red trailor, wondered about Nancy. The old lady's words in the gondola, scarcely listened to at the time, had echoed in her head; had come to rankle; had finished by seething like maggots in a dead woman's skull. "What's the use? The embrace, then the domestication. Later another embrace, rapidly domesticated." Something like that. Amedea pressed her lips tight, got the coupling straight, set the vehicles down, gave them a little push. "Rather boring, don't you feel?" Nancy had asked. Words, maggots, fish-bait. "Why this vulgar hankering after certainties?"

Indeed, indeed. Why? That wasn't what Amedea wanted at all! She knew she didn't. She had tried – oh, just tried – imagining Gérard living in the house at the Miracoli instead of Guy. The idea had been abominable. Not a marriage, nothing like a marriage! she prayed – and laughed again, a happy laughter this time, because she was on her knees praying, wasn't that funny? but Francesca looked at her oddly. A secret warmth! she prayed. An invisible light, a miraculous influence! It had been in hope of such a love that she had given Gérard her lagoon. There he was now, plodding wearily at his oar across it. Ah but why, then, had she thought of leasing that house in Tuscany? Oh, they might be glad of a bolt-hole. (They were two clichés, they would have a love affair.) And she was a fool, a fool, she had let herself imagine what Gérard might be like in Tuscany in middle age. Just imagine . . . Would he take to wearing cardigans and drinking gin and French and writing about the Sienese school?

Here was the graveyard island, its red brick walls, cypress grove. Guy was rowing her steadily by. He looked so gaunt these days! and dour! Easily he could be Death's oarsman, easily! Charon in a calico hat with a puggree. Had she made him so grim? For she had treated him vilely, she knew. That dinner outside La Fenice when he had made himself tell her he still loved her, how he longed for her to turn back to him, love him once more. And she had hesitated; hesitated; seconds had ticked; and then she had begun, "It's sad . . ." Had stopped again. Had tried to be honest. Tried to be brave. Failed. Finished, "It's sad – the arbour has died. *Le patron* was telling me. They're going to have to cut it down."

Here were the dead. Guy and she would lie here . . .

She had gone back to Nancy, but it hadn't done any good. The day of the Vogalunga it had been. Nancy had invited a dozen friends to her terrace to watch the boats approach the finish along her reach of the Grand Canal. Amedea had taken Corrado – she wanted him to see the painted barges, the banners, all the pageantry. When he was bigger, when he was twelve maybe, he and his father and she would row the Vogalunga in the *s'ciopon*, she had promised him, standing him on the balustrade so he could see.

She had stood holding the back of the child's shirt in case he wobbled. (When he grew up and they could talk about these things, would he begrudge her the happiness of her love affair if happiness it proved to be? She couldn't believe he would. But truly it was a relief her mother was not still alive to carp.) Then before they left she had managed to have Nancy a moment to herself. "When we were in your boat, darling, talking about love affairs," she had asked, "do you remember? What was it you meant about the hankering after certainties?"

But Nancy Goncharov had been in a different mood. "Oh, you mustn't cast me as your evil genius, my dear, I shouldn't like that." Painfully she had inched round in her chair, so she could include one or two of her other guests in her smile. "Do you know something glorious I discovered?" The story came in wisps of laughter. "My dears, a lady who used to live in this house before me . . . Oh, years ago . . . The turn of the century. Well . . ." Her decrepit eyebrows fought upward through a snowfall of powder on her forehead. "Along with works of art in the drawing-room, she had works of nature. Rather impressive ones. A leopard. A boa constrictor, I believe. A curious person," Nancy pondered, "she must have been. Naturally the poor things had to be subdued. Every few hours, a footman with a needle came. Apparently she liked the brutes sleepy, but not comatose." Nancy sipped her champagne. Then she reached out a slow hand for Amedea's sleeve, whispered in her ear, "When I think of that lady, I feel wonderfully virtuous . . . I with only my silly cake house."

Hopeless, Nancy had been, Amedea thought, as now side by side the *s'ciopon* and the *sandolo* left the open water, came into Venice. Hopeless and charming and mischievous Nancy had been.

Sitting on the thwart, Amedea dumped her elbows on her knees, bowed her head. She had not rowed. But she was weary, weary. And it was curious, ever since Nancy had told her the story of the leopard in the drawing-room, she had been imagining herself at Nancy's age. She would not, she thought, make a bad old lady. One of those infirm grandes dames who get sought out and pampered by art historians; who swagged in family jewellery totter escorted forth to a cocktail party now and then; who have outlived most of those who loved them and most of their capacity for love, but give their hangers-on amusing value for their sycophancy, then go to earth again in their grimy *palazzi*. But Amedea could only imagine herself old now, not in 2020 say. What would Venice be like then? Never a word of Venetian spoken in the schools or the shops. A tourist resort, a museum, with the houses occupied off and on by the rich from Milan, Munich, Philadelphia. But that wasn't the point. Why, why, when she imagined herself old, did she always see herself solitary like Nancy Goncharov? No husband. No lover. Not even her son – what had happened to Corrado in these dreams? An old lady, ridiculous naturally, but game; gallant in her way; kindling when taken to a party; nettled when not invited. But solitary always. It made her nervous. It depressed her.

So the boats came home as the sun reached its height.

"You've had your lunch," Signora Donatella said, hitching the hammock between the bay tree and the pomegranate tree, "now you must sleep."

"Can I come to the Festa?" Corrado wanted to know.

She had swung him up, deposited him in the hammock. If he wriggled hard he could make his boat of rope netting rock till it nearly capsized. Soon she would order him not to tip himself out, not to be a little idiot, the ground was hard.

"If you sleep for an hour you can come to the Festa. Now lie still and close your eyes."

"The fireworks?"

"They're very late, the fireworks. We'll have to see. Perhaps if you're extremely good." And to Francesca Ziani, who was coming out into the garden as she went in, Donatella grunted, "His mother is off gallivanting somewhere."

In the greenery, birds were scuffling and cheeping. Here was Francesca, standing beside his hammock. "Look," she said, and pointed.

He looked. Alongside his hammock was a patch of the garden wall where no ivy had grown. And there were his geckoes, Francesca was right, there they were, one two three four of them, little grey things clinging to the wall.

It was an old, an honoured sport of his, gecko-watching. (Francesca had faith in its soporific potency.) They didn't stir, except their grey sides panted. Were they asleep? If they were awake, would they tumble off the wall if they fell asleep?

Corrado wondered which one would scuttle first, guessed at the second scuttler, closed his eyes.

Everyone who had a vessel went afloat at the Festa del Redentore. Families went aboard their *San Pierotte*, sallied forth with awnings, with hampers for supper on the water, with lanterns for nightfall. It appeared that all the friends and lovers in the wreck of the Serene Republic were out sculling their *sandoli* and *mascarete*. There were merry voices and pretty dresses and straw hats on every canal.

Francesca Ziani stood on board Mauro Zanier's *bragozzo*, helped Mauro and his wife lay a table on deck for the party that evening. Table cloth, knives and forks, glasses, even napkins, Lord what luxury. Etienne Maas and Franco Tagliapietra were coming; and the Zanier children of course; and people Francesca didn't know; and Donatella, Corrado, the kitten Strassa; and Guy she supposed, and Amedea and Gérard she supposed. Straightening her back – they had been lifting cases of wine into the hold – Francesca saw the blue and grey *sandolo* (oh why couldn't she have happened not to notice it?) slip away from the Giudecca southward.

The faithful were swarming sluggishly across the bridge of boats that conscripts had moored from the Zattere to the Redentore where mass after mass was being said. On the Lido in the garden of the Hotel des Bains, when the afternoon breeze failed, Jazz Age palm trees shimmied to a standstill, let their bangs fall in their eyes. Away on Sant'Erasmo a smallholder's fire of lopped scrub plumed smoke up into the blue. The sacrifice must have been pleasing, because across the tideway, in the sky over San Nicolò, brilliant parachutes were revealed, drifted down toward the beach.

It is happening, Francesca thought. One stands here laying out spoons because Caterina Zanier, bless her, has made an enormous *tirami su*; one stands here knowing about the Des Bains palm trees because after frittering years away on this lagoon one cannot not know about their shimmying; knowing also for instance that on the island of Sacca Sessola the old caretaker will be scything beneath his acacia trees and pear trees because he always seems to be doing that whenever I chance to row by; and knowing that it is happening. It. It. Because if as somebody or other said – why the devil can't I remember names? – the death of a mouse from cancer is the whole sack of Rome by the Goths, then the slipping away southward of that *sandolo* right now is a rending of the firmament, a –

"I can't imagine!" she despaired laughingly to Caterina, who had asked her how on earth they could persuade the ice in the red plastic tub to melt more gradually. She would, she resolved abruptly, write her thesis about Italo Svevo when the time came. But no, no, it wasn't Svevo who had said that about the mouse with cancer. Who?

Despite the lack of wind, every vessel that had a sail had hoisted it. Tan sails, white sails, blue sails, sails with fantastic heraldic designs, drifted slowly by, mirrored in the calm lagoon. The *bragozzo* had pushed off from the quay now, the party was under way, bottles were being uncorked, Corrado was towing *Hispaniola* astern. Working barges had been swabbed, had been bedecked with lanterns and flowers. In the holds, the bargees had shipped trestle tables and chairs; their wives, parents, children, cousins would dine in lagoon grandeur. Just south of the Giudecca, boys and girls were swimming off a hulk foundered in the shallows. A grandmother in black had been marooned on the tarred wreck to keep an eye on them. She had been humanely marooned – she had her knitting and a kitchen chair.

Francesca shaded her eyes with her hand. The dot which was the *sandolo* she had seen launched that morning had reached Sacca Sessola. The caretaker of the abandoned hospital would lean a minute on his scythe, look up at the swans creaking and soughing overhead. Usually he had the thickets and swamps to himself, lived alone among the dragonflies and warblers darting over the sedge. Only lovers and fishermen came occasionally sculling south from Venice to plant an oar in the shoal and tie up to it. He must be looking at the *sandolo* now, thinking they were lovers probably, seeing they didn't stop.

The *sandolo* crept away like an insect over the lagoon. Helplessly Francesca imagined its progress. She had Guy

Ashmanhaugh at her side, the *bragozzo*'s helm in his right hand, main-sheet in his left, pretending he knew no ill, imagined nothing, pretending like her. Now the *sandolo* was passing San Clemente. Francesca knew Codussi's locked church that basked there. She knew the tablet on the church wall, moss furring the flaws, with some naval victory carved in relief, galleons streaming pennants, galleys locking banks of oars. There was a standpipe too, with cold clean water welcome to oarsmen on sweaty days. Very likely Amedea and Gérard were stopping to splash their faces, to cup their hands and drink. Francesca was wiping ice cream off Corrado's chin, she had to imagine San Clemente, which she could see moored out there on the blue, she had to bring it close to her eyes. The madhouse beside the church, its rows of neoclassical windows glittering. By law all the madhouses had been shut. But no other provision for the crazy had been made, so in a few of the noble rooms at San Clemente spectral men and women still lay in stupor on beds, sat in stupor on chairs. An island, a palace, a garden – it wasn't a bad gaol. And to have your church by Codussi, even if it were never opened, and sparrows flustering in its eaves – not bad, Francesca thought. Though doubtless Amedea and Gérard would feel haunted momentarily if as they rowed on south they saw one of the wraiths pottering along a gravel path beneath the trees, coming to cling to the gate, stare out through the bars across the water. But perhaps they would only see a solid, capable nurse in reassuring white step out a moment into the sun on the quay.

It was happening. A mouse was dying of cancer. This was the end of life at the house at the Miracoli as Francesca had known it. Cruelty, ruin had come in. She swigged her glass of wine, refilled it, sipped. Everyone on board the *bragozzo* was extraordinarily calm. Etienne was being jovial, saying "Let me help" to Mauro, hoiking corks out of bottles with terrific jerks of his blue-shirted, leg-of-mutton arm. "Amedea wanted to try out Gérard's new boat," Guy was remarking. "I expect they'll join us for dinner." His marriage might make a partial recovery. Very likely, Francesca thought, it would live on a ghastly long time, an invalid, a poor thing. And certainly his courage this evening was more than she could bear, now the *sandolo* had reached Poveglia.

Her sacred island, Amedea called Poveglia. Her circle of green and quietness, she called it – inaccurately, though that would never bother her, because there was a creek cutting through, the place was two irregular splotches of green. She had used to row there with her father sometimes. Poveglia. Of course. Where else would you take a lover in the southern lagoon? Francesca demanded of Strassa, picking her up because now three people had very nearly trodden on her, then holding the little pitchy creature to her face because suddenly she had stupid, nervous, hot tears in her eyes. Porto di San Leonardo where the tankers moor, for pity's sake? Santo Spirito which is nothing but ruins and rubble, though once in the church there a Titian hung?

Cruelty had not come into the Miracoli house before, but it had now. Guy's self-control had not been a mockery before, but it was now. On the tideway at Poveglia the sun would be beating down and dazzling and beating up. A barge or two, a yacht using her engine maybe. Gulls that flew up from the *briccole* that marked the channel, or stretched their wings and shat but didn't fly. Scummy tide slithering seaward over the shoals. Fraying fish floating belly-up, clots of fraying brown weed rubbing against the gulls' rotting posts. Then the island trees, the *campanile* with its bricked-up arches, the rusty water-tower . . . "You really must look after your kitten," Francesca admonished her second cousin – who would not be five for several months even if his godfather had already produced a pair of ebony hair brushes with his initials on their backs, who was too young to be reasonably expected to remember all Strassa's requirements. "Do you think she's hungry?"

Poveglia had a hospital too – nineteenth-century and ruined, this one. Dead elms. Living cedars, tamarisks, figs. A ruined boathouse. They must have sculled into the weedy creek behind the stump of the old fortress. It was swathed with brambles – you got a good blackberry crop later in the year. No doubt the smell of high summer foliage swam on the lagoon smells of stagnancy, cicadas churred, mosquitoes whined.

There was no caretaker living on Poveglia. Just an old man who rowed over from Malamocco to tend the vineyard, feed the abandoned dogs. With him, the dogs were quiet. But Francesca had once stumbled through the thickets as far as the dozing pack and they had made a shindy as if a dead fool going down to the Styx and having nothing better to do had kicked Cerberus. She had retreated briskly, blundered into a nettle-bed. Amedea had laughed at her.

Now Amedea must be leading Gérard by the hand, shoving through the undergrowth behind the old laundry, among collapsing administrative ranges and wards. Not much in those buildings any more, except iron heaters big as donkeys. Elder grew up to the lintels; ivy straggled right over the roofs. In the arcade there were swallows' nests. Would Amedea show him the wrecked hospital library where the shelves were smashed for kindling decades back, show him the mound on the floor, the mouldering mound of thrillers and religious tracts? Tell him about the dead? She had told Francesca about the dead. How as a girl in a ward where half the roof had fallen she had come upon them – the dead. A huddle of nineteenth-century wheelchairs. The dead sitting in them. "Honestly, Francesca, I thought I saw them!" They had been dreaming their deaths away a long while; some of them could remember Manin's rebellion, Amedea had assured her, laughing, elaborating. They sat staring out of broken windows at pollards, nettles, gnats. What did they talk about? Oh, local gossip. First nights at La Fenice. Wildfowling. The winter the lagoon froze.

Francesca knelt down with a saucer of scraps for the kitten. This was about all she was good for, according to Amedea, she thought. It was about her level – laying spoons because there would be *tirami su*, wiping ice-cream off childish chins, that kind of thing. While Guy and Mauro and Etienne with glasses in their hands – and Guy still had the big oak tiller against his hip – were discussing what maintenance work the *bragozzo* would need next winter, glancing away occasionally to enjoy the lagoon evening's blues and pinks and golds. And in the quiet, grassy courtyard on Poveglia no doubt Amedea was at last putting her arms around Gérard's neck and kissing him – she would have to seduce him, he would not first lay a finger on her – with bravura, oh fine actressy stuff, classy stuff, Francesca thought, standing up because Strassa had started to nibble.

"You are very lovely this evening," Franco Tagliapietra told her. "Not obvious beauty like your cousin's, but . . ." (Good God, the girl had tears in her eyes – they were brimming; brown and brimming; and wide, wide.) "If I were to paint either of you, I should choose you." (Vaguely he had heard that she had had a fling with Gérard Charry. But she wasn't in love with him too, was she? Oh poor child, poor child!) "But I can't paint the human figure. I never could."

It had been revolting, Francesca's heart protested, the way Amedea and Gérard had brought the *sandolo* alongside the *bragozzo*, had come on board for dinner. Her kisses for her son, her ticklings for his kitten, her blandishments for his frowning nanny – all revolting.

Or perhaps it was right that those with a magnificent capacity for happiness should with a little good fortune and a little ruthlessness satisfy it – or the world would be even sadder than it was. Was it reasonable, Amedea's assumption that to take a lover was behaviour far from extraordinary, behaviour everyone was to accept instantly, have no opinion of at all? For almost no one feasting on the *bragozzo* anchored off San Giorgio Maggiore could doubt what those hours on Poveglia meant, Francesca had been sure. There were Amedea's debonair laugh and her flickery eyes to betray her; Gérard's quietness and distractedness and politeness to betray him. Nobody had paid any attention. (But a mouse was dying of cancer. Ruin had entered the house.) While the skiff tied alongside bumped gently; and all around, in the sunset on the lagoon, voices and laughter rose from anchored craft, and lanterns were lit . . .

Guy Ashmanhaugh and Gérard Charry had sought each other out. Military service they had talked about (those recruits who had built the bridge of boats); Palladio they had talked about; algae they had talked about . . . passing the cold chicken, the tomato salad. They had parts to play, Francesca had supposed, astounded. Perhaps they truly were all right, lifting their forks from their plates to their mouths, listening, swallowing, saying the next thing – about Donizetti for some reason, then *La Stampa*, was the book page well done?

I am only nineteen, I comprehend nothing, Francesca had decided in despair. How even could she condemn her cousin for beginning to satisfy her heart's desire or whatever it was? She looked innocent enough, leaning to light someone's cigarette. Was it her fault if she had grown into her capacity for love only this year? This business was a massacre of the innocents by the innocents, Francesca had thought. Probably people who were married often had love affairs; she was nineteen; she didn't know; perhaps it didn't matter that much; she would learn. Though at Etienne Maas' dance later that evening her heart was still protesting: They have stopped work on the Tower of Babel. Oh the fools, the fools! The most magnificent enterprise of all has been abandoned. Wretches to give up so easily! For the love between man and woman, a love instituted and evident, a love that delighted in the world and that the world could delight in – was this not an undertaking worth doggedness? Fools! For of course it was Guy's fault too. He had given up.

Francesca leaned on Etienne's studio balcony. On the quay below, the crowd was dining at hundreds of tables. Out on the Giudecca Canal the quick lights of motorboats and the slow lights of rowing boats jigged on the black water. The bridge of boats still bore thick, slow currents of the pious and the festive. She looked beyond, to the lighters anchored out in Bacino di San Marco, the lighters where the fireworks would be sent up. On their gloomy decks she could make out tiny figures with torches working. And yes, luckily her pride had come back. At nineteen she was as old as Venice and as knowing. (Anyhow, at her age some girls were married, weren't they?) For no one, no one on board the *bragozzo* had said one true word except her. She had stood with tears in her eyes and started mumbling to Franco Tagliapietra, "Sorry, stupid of me . . ." But then she had got a grip on her cowardice, wrestled it overboard, stood upright without it, the *victrix*, and asked, "I can cry for someone, can't I?" And Franco had regarded her and then nodded and then smiled. So that now she rather felt that he would not be always trying to cajole her to his studio, cuddling her, suggesting hauling her clothes off; but they might be friends.

"Do you always shake when someone asks you how you are?" Ralph Chedgrave enquired with his voice that when he was forty seemed to have broken a second time, gone down another register to bitter depths below the common run of men.

Help! Francesca besought the night air – jittery, because unseen approaches had always frightened her, it was silly but she couldn't help it. And Ralph had spoken in English (she had the vaguest notion of his meaning), and his Italian was disgraceful, and her English worse, so how could they speak?

"Do you remember . . . ?" she managed to wonder aloud

in English. But what might the formidably rich Signor Chedgrave (or were they his debts that were formidable? had she heard there was some obscurity?) care to remember? And what words for whatever it was could she muster? Ah but there stood his Savile Row trouser legs to rescue her! "That time you and I came out of Gino's Bar, Ralph, remember?" she pronounced gingerly in Italian. Was he with her? His eyes looked as if he knew what she was saying. "*Acqua alta* had come up, there was a foot of water in the street. Your shoes and trousers were too beautiful, you didn't want to wade home." She stooped, she was aghast for his Prince of Wales check, she laughed, she acted rolled-up trousers, acted wading. "Then we saw a young *facchino* pushing a barrow. You yelled Gondola! and the fellow grinned and stopped."

"Was he a good-looking porter?" Ralph had got the idea, he spoke slow English. But his weariness with himself sounded, Francesca thought, like a trunk being dragged across a floor. It was nerve-wracking to try to understand. And he must be so unhappy, to have developed that voice! "I'm sure I wouldn't have yelled Gondola! if he wasn't."

"He was very good-looking. I was jealous," she promised him in Italian. But now he was staring bloodshotly straight through her face, through her mind without seeing anything there, out through the back of her skull. "You splashed across to his barrow. I worried about your trouser legs. Don't you remember, Ralph? On the barrow you turned around. You sprawled feet up and head down, like St Peter being crucified."

"No doubt . . ." (grate, in English, of a trunk being dragged) "so I could . . ." (grate of amusement that he despised himself so justly) "watch the lad . . ." (grate that may simply have been decades of alcohol and tobacco) "shoving me along."

"Yes, that's what I thought. Don't you remember?"

"No. Nothing at all. And I don't believe a word you've said." *What* was he saying? *Could* he be? She blushed; leaned closer; harked. "That's the kind of story . . . girls like you . . . make up about me."

Etienne save me! Francesca prayed. You who have painted the pictures and hung them on the walls. You who command the view over the Giudecca Canal and the old Muranese glass lights and the easel and the piano and the dancers. You who in the other studio next door command the vast etching press with its spokes and sheen and precision. You who ordained supper in the kitchen for those who had not got around to eating earlier in the night. Who ordained that flamboyant creature cavorting in fish-net tights and a tail coat and a red mouth. Save me. I cannot stand here forever beside Ralph, and he will not dance with me or take me out in a boat to watch the fireworks.

And Etienne Maas came. (Everyone's nerves were a bit frayed this evening, he reflected, what with Guy's and Amedea's marriage at last summoning the courage of its convictions and lying down to die. And Francesca Ziani was sweet, and she had been trying hard all evening, and she was only a girl.) He had ordained Tiziana Valier swirling her skirts – her family owned a department store, she was a carefree soul. He had ordained Federico Trevisan who once had leaped out of an hotel window. (The girl had not confessed she was married till a male fist started bludgeoning the bedroom door, but then she hissed Jump! jump! and Federico broke his feet, he still danced with a limp.) He had ordained Cecilia Zancana whose black curls were irresistible; whose laughter was ceaseless despite the fact that she had been ditched by Gérard Charry – and there Gérard was, dancing with Amedea; Cecilia who had got engaged when she was absurdly young – to the son of her father's stockbroker, Francesca had heard – one of those interminable engagements that extinguished all zest, but she didn't seem to be up to breaking it. He had ordained a detachment of English girls . . .

All these things Etienne Maas had done; Francesca recognised it, watching his rolling gait as he proceeded toward her through his guests. But she would not tease him about his English girls, or only gently. About how it was one of his life's inexplicable marvels, the way the English moneyed classes dispatched their daughters to Italy to study the language or the art or whatnot, always with ribands in their hair, always longing to meet a real artist – Francesca would not tease him roughly. Nor about how he liked his English girls aristocratic for preference – his erotic snobbery was the most harmless and comic of vices – and had he not been penniless, a nobody, till he sold his first canvas? In short, the Honourable Julia on his left and the Honourable Victoria on his right Francesca would forgive Etienne instantly and outright, because he had reached her side. "Come and dance," he commanded. He would save her from Death leaning on his scythe – well, not exactly, but from Ralph Chedgrave who was Death leaning on an easel. "Then we're going out in the *bragozzo* to watch the fireworks."

Those were the *anni di piombo*, the terrorist years. Up and down Italy people were being kidnapped, maimed, killed. But not in Venice, which had failed to keep step with the century, where contemptible hedonists could dance the nights away and not bother, Amedea Lezze thought standing at her oar in the darkness, to read in their newspapers the next day about whom the Red Brigades had shot.

When with a whoosh and a crackle the first rocket went up, the hundreds of boats fell quiet, fell still. Gérard sat on the thwart, his hands, which ached from rowing most of the day, curled half-open on his knees. But Amedea stood very upright, plying her oar softly, just stirring it in the water enough to stop the *sandolo* being carried by the tide dangerously close to the lighters; and when high above her the rocket exploded and shook its scarlet and golden parasols over the bay she knew she had never felt so exalted before, never felt love like this. In the flashing firework-light, Palladio's churches and the Dogana and the Palazzo Ducale sprang into clarity and faded again. Amedea wanted to cry. She wanted to spend all tomorrow making love and drinking champagne. She didn't know what she wanted. (She is standing as one stands while the "Marseillaise" is played, her lover thought, she stands robed in glory. He would wait a short, ecstatic time, she would put off that robe, he would take her in his arms.) Venice had never been so fragile and so vulnerable, Amedea rejoiced, as in those febrile skyfuls of red, blue, green, silver, gold. The cannonade on the lighters roared; the night reverberated; her blood drummed. (In the watching armada Francesca, sitting on the dewy deck of the *bragozzo*, caught sight of the blue and grey *sandolo* for an instant; she thought, That is passion, and felt bleak; but then that firework went out.)

Some of the fireworks were designed to float when they fell. A flotilla of tiny fire-ships, Amedea thought, come to panic Venice and burn her fleet . . . But then in rapture because the peril was only a pretty game, her festive old Venice was safe tonight and looking ghostlily beautiful, she asked, "Did you have a Swiss Army knife when you were a boy?" and laughed, because Gérard looked surprised when he answered, "Yes, I think I've still got it somewhere."

It was too exhausting – how could she explain? Of course she ought to explain. Wasn't he her . . . oh all that? (Instantly – why? – she had collapsed, all exhilaration gone.) Ah hell, he wouldn't understand. What was the good? But how momentarily she had seen one of those red knives with lots of blades, a pair of scissors, a corkscrew, she didn't know, a spike, gadgets for everything.

"Why?" Gérard smiled.

She couldn't remember. What had gone wrong in her? A Swiss Army knife, a red knife with lots of . . . Oh yes. Just a silly idea. For a moment, her love had felt like one of those knives, it could do far more than she could ever want.

Tired. And empty. Gutted. And she couldn't say anything so – so . . .

"Nothing." She shook her head. "Another time."

Guy Ashmanhaugh did not go to Etienne's dance. Carrying Corrado, he walked home to the Miracoli, Signora Donatella puffing beside him burdened with *Hispaniola* and Strassa.

Corrado declared again and again that he wanted to stay up to watch the fireworks, but when they laid him on his bed he fell asleep. Donatella gave Guy a steady look, and said "God bless you," and went to her bedroom.

Guy could not think what to do. He took a bottle of wine and a glass up to the *altana*, leaned on the wooden rail, waited for the fireworks, looked at them when they started showing away over the roofs. He tried to think, but nothing much came. You made your marriage of small, innocent things, of rituals the two of you shared; but rituals became empty forms. You made yourself out of small, innocent observances, some of which existed so tenuously that not even the wife you loved could see them; but they became a mockery too. What else was there to think?

Guy went down to the kitchen, fetched another bottle of wine, went out into the garden. He thought he might take that wasps' nest. Night was the best time to do it. Not that he disliked wasps. But with Corrado scampering about . . .

The nest was under the bay tree. He must get a spade, boil a kettle because he had forgotten to buy cyanide. The trouble was, boiling water did not always torture a whole nest to death; some might survive, have to be killed the following night. Ah, he would let the wasps wait for half an hour. First he would drink another glass of wine. This Venegazzu was really extremely good.

He was still sitting in a wicker chair in the unlit garden toward dawn when Francesca let herself in through the street door. He spoke her name, so as not to startle her if in the moonlight she saw his dark shape. Slowly she approached him. She had felt miserable after the firework show, she said, but Claudia Glaven had been a darling, not frightening at all, had taken her back to Ca' Zante, tried to cheer her up. (I have wept for you, she wanted to say, but could not.) They had gone up to the top floor, to the library, she told him, and sat on the sill and leaned against Lombardo's columns and dangled their legs over the Grand Canal.

So Claudia has been nice to the girl, Guy thought. Claudia and he had been friends since London years, though she had been much more glamorous than him. Married to one rock star, working for a second, in love, if he remembered rightly, with a third; while he had been a mere student of architecture. But they had become friends. And now, after some kind and worldly soothing of Francesca – whom other people's desires and despairs sent into swings and roundabouts of emotion, he thought, jaundiced, made her want to talk talk talk – Claudia had very likely gone back to sitting on the library window sill. Yes, she was probably thinking of him, Guy thought, of the decay of his marriage. Sorrowing for him, hoping for him – for they had been friends for years – on the library window sill.

He hoped Francesca was not going to want to be confided in now, want to express some feeling or other. No, luckily she was saying good night, moving toward the house. Then she came scurrying back, bent over him where he sat. With wet cheeks and an uncertain mouth she kissed him on his temple; she mumbled something or other; then she was gone.

Guy drank his wine. When he crossed his legs, wicker creaked. He thought in a fitful way – not much – India – Burma – anything except Amedea. Or was he dreaming? Damn, he'd spilled his wine.

There would be plenty of time to concentrate on Amedea's activities. Years. Concentrate on the fact that the marriage which for him had been the highest happiness he was capable of had been for her a time of slack feelings that later she transcended. Concentrate . . .

A girl. Good. Yes. That Burmese girl in Rangoon church – off Pagoda Road wasn't it? Red brick church, Victorian, corrugated iron roof, frangipani trees. His parents had been married there, he had gone to have a look.

The girl. She had been practising on the piano, was that it? She said she would switch on the fans. Those big old propellers in the roof began to churn. Burmese girls put sandalwood on their cheeks. Would he like to go up the tower? Key. Rungs, grime. At the belfry they stood on the shady side. There was a breeze. They looked down on all Rangoon and the plains and Rangoon river flowing to the sea. All the kingdoms of the earth.

Years afterward, in the garden of the Lezze house in Venice, the black kitten Strassa stalked the first sparrow of the day. It flew off. Under the bay tree, wasps began to fly up from their nest.

THREE

"I've been in Campo Santa Margherita with Corrado," Francesca Ziani said. "Then Guy took him off somewhere, I don't know where, I . . . A surprise for his birthday, I have an idea. Oh dear, perhaps it would have been better if he . . ."

"Don't worry." Her cousin laughed through her nose. "On the telephone I told Guy not to make a song and dance about my being here." The girl still had that habit of knitting her chubby fingers, she observed, knitting and knitting anxiously.

The nervous place to sit in the *salone* of the Miracoli house had always been the marquetry chair beneath the looking-glass, and Amedea homed in on it, Francesca noticed, seeing her lean the back of her head against the glass. It must feel cold.

"Those afternoons," Amedea laughed through her nose again, "of women and children in squares."

Whenever the weather wasn't too vile, Santa Margherita and San Polo came alive with palavering women and romping children. This was a Venice ritual too humble for Amedea Lezze ever to have taken to it much. Francesca on the contrary rather liked it.

Usually Signora Donatella escorted Corrado to play with his friends, but her chest was a lot worse this autumn; so sometimes Francesca deserted the university – and who today would have stayed indoors for yet another lecture on Futurism, for pity's sake, or on Hermeticism? only dolts. Because although it had been cold even in the sun, the air had been sheer light unmixed with any opacities, if she'd been out on the northern lagoon she'd have seen the Dolomites clearly today. So cold had it been toward the November sunset that Francesca had found herself alone apart from Corrado and the little friend entrusted to her care that afternoon who were scourging around with a ball.

She had huddled her coat to her ribs, she had paced up and down, she had not minded being alone. Indeed it had been something of a relief, after milder days when strangers politely mistook her for Corrado's mother and she had to explain, a very limited explanation which she hated uttering; or friendly women who were conversant with the whole scandal explained, usually volubly, usually just out of her earshot; or friendly women bullied her with advice about looking after a child; or she had to hear Corrado enlighten one of his companions, "That isn't my mother, that's Francesca."

Next spring the women and children would return to the squares. She would be twenty then. But nothing much else about the future could she predict. Would she sit some afternoons at café tables and drink coffee with amiable women and feel a trifle bored sometimes (but it would be agreeable in the spring sunshine) and a trifle guilty that she was not bending to her books (but Corrado needed her) and get up occasionally to put children with scratched knees back on diminutive bicycles? It depended on other people.

It depended on so many things. It seemed scarcely at all to depend on her. And when she had finished her degree? One day she might get married, have children of her own – she hoped she would. But could she abandon Corrado? Four months now since he last saw Amedea. And he didn't need any more betraying or teasing, Francesca had mused, noticing that the restoration of the tower of the Carmini was finished at last, and the statue of the Mother of God, which had been struck by lightning, which had attracted the lightning from the skies and conducted it blasting down the brick tower, was being hauled up again. She had checked in her pacing. The Madonna was in a cage, and the men when they stopped work had left her hanging halfway up the tower, hung in chains.

Then here had come Nancy Goncharov's old gondolier. "Good evening, Signor Alvise." "Good evening, Francesca." One day he had stopped and chatted nostalgically – since Nancy's death, he had got rather mournful – and he was fond of Francesca who was, he said, left over from the old days even if she was still only a sweet maid, and he called her *vecia* to show his affection – but today he had stumped on, perhaps because of the glassy air, the cold. She had gone on keeping an eye on the rampaging children; gone on waiting for Guy Ashmanhaugh, who was at a meeting with a client nearby; gone on dreading Amedea's appearance that evening, but longing for it too, fascinated naturally. Then Franco Tagliapietra on his way somewhere had noticed her, had swerved from his straight line across the square. He had taken the trouble to smile, to say something about the Madonna in irons on the tower wall before he walked on – so in a hazy way they both knew that he would always be there if she ever wanted him, though she never would.

Francesca had been alone again. The sun had gone below the roofs. In the square which was a trough of dusk now she had gently kicked the children's ball with them. What with it being his fifth birthday, and his mother coming, there was a distinct risk of Corrado getting over-excited, she had thought, trying to keep the charging and the hacking good-humoured. The wintry sunset behind Mary hanged from her tower, that dark blue sky, those crimson fires, those gold fires – these Francesca could tell Amedea about. And about Corrado's friend Armando, and what scamps they were, yes. But about what it felt like caring for Corrado who was not her child but truly she believed she loved as if he were . . . ? What it felt like waiting for Guy whom she loved dearly but who so rarely opened his heart to her even a little . . . ? (Were they any closer to each other after these last four ghastly months? If so, they were moving together about as trippingly as two tectonic plates.)

No, these were not things Francesca could speak of now. And yet she ought to try. For honesty's sake. Well, conceivably if courage came . . . or at some distant time, like when she was twenty . . .

"I expect they'll be back soon," she said. "And Donatella – she went with them. Would you . . . Would you like a drink?" But then she blushed, because it couldn't be right to play the hostess to that guest in that house.

What about her husband's nosebleeds, Francesca wondered, was that the kind of thing Amedea might wish to know about? She stopped stock-still in the kitchen with a corkscrew in her hand. Once she had come in, found Guy flat on his back on that table, Donatella's cooking things shoved aside, the old woman bending over his face, taking away his sodden red handkerchief, giving him a wad of paper ones. Francesca thought some wives might have been interested in this event, but perhaps not Amedea Lezze.

And the way that Guy, seeing Donatella stand at his head and she at his feet, had smiled and said, "You look like acolytes." How she then had been afraid, because it was sinister how you could never feel the blood leaking in your head, only when it trickled outside, slid down your lips. Ah, she had thought. Now I understand. This is how it will be for Guy, for me, all of us. The mind gives us warning, this is how one day it will dribble away.

And Guy's headaches? They had become so frequent, so unmanning, he had given in to the interrogations of the girl he found himself sharing his house with – sharing a lot with – the task, for example, of recounting again and again to Corrado the splendid manner in which, at the siege of Seringapatam, the redoubtable Baron Munchausen caught the enemies' cannon-balls and threw them back at the fortress, thus demolishing the ramparts.

Francesca had now stood a bottle of Pinot Grigio on the table, she had balanced the corkscrew on the cork so it wobbled like a child dancer up on her points for the first time. But it did not seem that Francesca was going to push down and turn; she could not push and turn. There were two chief headaches, Guy had explained. One was when being in love with Amedea made him so sad he wanted to flop down on his knees, rock forward what seemed to be the battering pestle of consciousness and the empty mortar of the world till his brow touched the floor. Then the pestle of thought would bash about the mortar of his mind so violently, he would be afraid it might crash through, appear sticking out above one eye, say, or between the parietal bones where the fontanelles had been. Having explained this, he had at once become laconic. It was nothing of great account, his love. (Francesca, sitting listening, had pressed her knees together, had pressed her lips together, had twined her fingers.) It was just being in love in his married way, in his solid way, Guy had made clear. There were, no doubt, greater loves.

The other headache was when the problem in his head was a winch. A very normal winch, he had described, such as one might find on any Venetian slipway. An iron winch, with an electric motor. Years ago it had been given a coat of paint. Most of the time the winch slumbered in the boatyard, come rain, come shine, or performed its daily labours efficiently. But then things would go wrong – a chain would catch, would tighten round Guy's consciousness like a tourniquet. That usually occurred by day. (Francesca knew. She had seen him straying about the house unquietly, leaving doors open and lights shining, his hands at his forehead as if trying to free the snag.) But there was another trick the winch played, that prevented sleep, or if he slept it woke him floundering. The winch span around, faster and faster it paid out line, it was as if a harpooned whale were plunging away. His drum brain whirled, the tearaway warp of thought, of sanity, of his life, whipped out of his head, faster, faster, there couldn't be much line left, not much, none. With a destroying jolt, the line was ripped from its fastening on the floor of his brainpan. The snapped end flew away, snaked for a senseless instant in his sight, was gone. The idiot drum revolved a while, slowing. It stopped.

Guy had hoped rowing might help, so in the hall she had helped him scrape and sand the *s'ciopon.* Francesca made herself grip the neck of the bottle in her left fist, push and twist the corkscrew with her right (it was not a wobbly dancer now, it had become a cross being erected, the tortured man widening his arms to heaven); she remembered how cold it had been working on the boat in the hall. Guy would only paint at night, when Corrado and Signora Donatella were in bed. "Better than always going out," he had said. And he had stood a bottle and glasses on the hall bench. The October darkness had blown in off the canal with the drenched chill of death, Francesca had thought. And Guy had not lit a fire since Amedea had left him; no warm flame-light played on the fireplace's carved nymphs and satyrs. They had painted in a slapdash way, two coats instead of the usual four. In a week, the *s'ciopon* had been back on the canal, her skimped overhaul done.

Then Guy had rowed in all weathers. Once he had announced he was off to Murano to look at the restoration work being done on the mosaic floor of San Donato. And Francesca had not liked to say she would not come, just because if the rain being flung at the city got a degree or two colder it must surely be sleet that soused them. She had not even liked to suggest they catch a *vaporetto* like normal people did, though she had remarked, as the *s'ciopon* headed out across the lagoon and began to toss, as their oilskins billowed and the rain rinsed down their sou'westers, that she could not remember an autumn like it. At Murano they had moored their green skiff by the apse, gone inside. Like all the finest lagoon floors, it undulated. Their oilskins dripping, their feet splotching, they had gazed at those inlaid convolutions, these soft hues. A priest coming and going at the chancel end, a few old women on chairs – soon it would be vespers. The area of floor that had been taken up was roped off. Planks, mud, tools. The restorers had gone home. Guy had wandered; she had seen him try not to concentrate too hard, try to gaze casually. They had come out into the stormy nightfall. No luck, Guy had said: the peacocks, urns and flowers had stayed on the floor, hadn't risen into his head, hadn't helped.

Francesca pressed down on the heavenward arms of the crucified man, the cork rose out of the bottle. She was not impudently playing the hostess in her cousin's old house, she realised. The case was simpler. She was, as she went to the dresser for two glasses, just back to being Amedea's handmaiden.

Things she had done with Guy . . . Things, rituals, this and that. Walking home one night they had watched the first barges from the mainland tie up at the market quay. That had been a ceremony of Amedea's and his, hadn't it? she pondered uneasily, carrying the wine and the glasses through to the *salone*. To lean on the parapet of Rialto bridge, see the barges moor gunwhale to gunwhale. How by lantern-light the men lifted ashore the crates of fish and vegetables. To go down then to where they were rigging the awnings and tilts, day beginning to break, the last bats still ricocheting. To go into the first bars that open there for the market people and boat people, drink coffee that was generally chicory, drink a glass of grappa, eat the warm brioches.

Or . . . Look, Francesca demanded of Amedea silently, can you imagine this? A man and a woman. At a landing stage. Waiting for a boat. Can you see us? (She put a glass of wine on the ormolu table beside her cousin's braceleted wrist.) Can you imagine us? Untouching. Never touching. The lagoon dusk came down in an exhausted sort of way. But the pale, wavering strip of air between the two coats didn't look as if anyone would ever want to close it. We had forgotten the ferry timetable, or mistimed our walk. The wait took a long time.

That was on the landing stage at Ca' La Vela on the island of Sant'Erasmo. Yes, I've been trespassing on ground that Guy shared with you. (Ah but would Amedea feel disposed to tell her about Tuscany, about Gérard? Francesca had seen him two or three times that autumn, rowing about Venice alone. He had waved, but he hadn't stopped.) But we might have been on any quay where ferries tie up. Or on any of the unreckonable landing stages on forgotten stretches where no ferry goes. Or on one of the abandoned islands. Places we needed the *s'ciopon* to get to. Creeks twisting and turning to inexistence in marsh somewhere.

Evenings have often found us turning for home. August, September, October, November. There we have been, waiting on jetty after jetty for ferries that seemed to have gone down with all hands, south in the Bacino di Chioggia or north by Lio Piccolo or somewhere . . . ferries vanished inexplicably behind a ruined church or a reedbed, so that waiting we shivered and yawned . . . ferries foundered where the hulk crewed by carcasses would rust on a muddy shoal of some *barena* till Venice were forgotten. Or we'd be shoving the *s'ciopon* off from trees and rubble and driftwood somewhere, turning the bow to where the city was lighting up in sparks and glows, beginning to shine over the lagoon. United by disappointment, we two, nothing more. (But if she were straight with her cousin, Francesca would have to confess that it was sobering how her passion for Gérard Charry had vanished into thin air. And last spring she had agonised, had longed! been on tenterhooks! Yes, it was sobering.) United, sundered . . . But no, there had been moments when she had felt united with Guy, however tenuously. Moments when she seemed to hear his silence murmuring: Nothing of this is worth much, but take it if it amuses you. Smoke from a cottage chimney. Goats cropping brackish scrub. Take them, he would seem to be saying, if you have a taste for these things. They used to delight Amedea and me, but now . . . "That day moon," he had said aloud once, "starting to look less wan. And Hesperus up in the west. Look, Francesca." But mostly it had been silent, his offering, and she might have imagined it. Just a way he had of turning to regard things. Mallard quacking overhead as they came flighting in. A watery sunset behind thorns on a sea-wall. A gunmetal pool.

Francesca sauntered to the French windows, turned. "There's so much I want to tell you!" she cried effusively. (For had not a mouse died of cancer? and had not falsity or wisdom entered her?) "But first you must tell me about Gérard – how is he? And about Tuscany! It must have been bliss, Tuscany. Absolute bliss . . ."

"No!" Amedea exclaimed, heaving her head away from the looking-glass. "Oh – I – I – I'm sorry."

Gérard Charry was not there to whisper in Francesca's ear that when Amedea seemed agitated or inarticulate it very likely meant merely that she was being, as she thought, like other people, and hoping to be cherished for it. (His Tuscan sojourn had served, if for nothing else, to confirm him in this belief.) So Francesca simply felt sorry for Amedea's distress, and felt confused. "*Wasn't* it bliss?" she asked, pulled up short in her tracks – for it had never occurred to her that Amedea and Gérard could fail to make a pretty paradisal adventure out of it. If her cousin wanted bliss, in Francesca's experience bliss was what she generally got. Then . . . ? "Oh I'm sorry," she mumbled in her turn. "You mean you don't want to talk about it?"

"No . . . No, it's not that." Amedea stood up, began to move aimlessly. She glanced at Strassa asleep on an armchair. She stepped over battered ships of her son's fleet moored alongside wharves built of books and Guy's old cigar boxes. "Oh, I don't *know*, Francesca. I will try to tell you. Later. Slowly."

But already Francesca was sure she understood. Was the child whom Amedea had abandoned not coming through the streets toward the house right now? was she not about to embrace him? No wonder she didn't want to tell stories about Tuscany! Stupid I am! Francesca accused herself. Unkind I am! Amedea's heart must be churning over and over like a cement-mixer, she must be listening . . .

Cold darkness stood flatly in the windows, would not come in because the chandelier was glimmering. The iron crash of a shop's shutters echoed. Then a barge going by below made the air shudder, left the slappings of its wake. Mist wisped through balcony balustrades. On a roof across the water, dilapidated aerials stood like ancient pines on a hill, or the crosses rotting on Golgotha. And there was silence now . . . No, Francesca thought, not quite. That faint humming, faint clicking, the susurrus of quietness she never knew was in the air, it might be in her brain, no, air, no, brain.

Under her breath, Amedea sang, *Are you still drinking in your stinking pink palazzo* . . . ? But she had given her house away. Given it to Guy in the hope of convincing him – had she succeeded? – that her promise not to separate Corrado and him, her promise to take upon herself not only the blame for a failed marriage but as much of the distress as possible too, was inviolable as her marriage vows had not been. She smiled her apologies for her restlessness. (And certainly would not oblige Francesca by immediately talking about Gérard.) "Tell me what's been happening here," she demanded. "The boat. Our friends."

Gérard Charry admired the smart rowing clubs like the Bucintoro and the Querini. He admired the way their boats were always in beautiful condition, the oarsmen always went afloat wearing their club colours. But the club along Fondamenta della Misericordia, which he had joined, was a small, poor club. There were only half a dozen *puparin* and *mascarete*, and none of them had been built by a first-class yard, by Amadi for instance, and they always needed a coat of paint. When the oarsmen put forth for a regatta, they all wore clothes of different colours, and they looked piratical with their trouser legs rolled up, sashes round their waists, scarves round their heads.

The club was called the Remo d'Oro and occupied a couple of rooms on the quay. Over the window it was written: VOGHEMO, CHE EL NOSTRO ONOR XE INCOMINCIÀ DAL REMO, exhorting Venetians to row because their glory had begun with the oar. The rooms were cluttered with cups, festooned with flags. Men from the workshops nearby went there in the evening, and the men from the yard where the funeral barges were moored, where they touched up the gold paint on the lions and urns. Gérard sometimes went there too, to drink a glass of wine, to talk about boats. Quite possibly he was there right now, Amedea thought.

His own boat he kept in a *squero* on Rio dell'Avogaria. There were a hoist for launching, a standpipe for washing boats down, a brazier for the vats of bubbling tar and for the men's fish at midday. The blue and grey *sandolo* lay on a trolley near the hoist. Other craft lay on trestles to be repaired or painted. Back beneath the timbered roof, hulls were stacked one on another. Disused gondolas were slung from the beams, lay in their ropes high in the dim temple like black arks of an obscure old covenant. Cats fought, slept, copulated, gave birth and died beneath foredecks, on rafters in the roof, on ledges running from bay to bay. Returning sometimes at night under the stars, Gérard and Amedea had heard them howling.

Still she didn't know whether she felt proud or guilty that now and then she had been in Venice for a day or two and had not seen Corrado. Had stayed in the Misericordia attic. Had gone away again, usually alone. Of course idyllic enough, she thought. Oh idyllic enough, to go winding along canal after canal with her lover on late summer nights, on early autumn nights, she heard her mind beginning to snarl. But these days Venice chiefly made her fretful. Already she was planning how Gérard and she should get away from Italy altogether. Anyhow for a few months. They would sail *Zenobia* to the Ionian, to the Aegean, next spring, next summer, she didn't know. But she wanted to get offshore. She dreamed of that threshold numinous to sailors where you cross from shore-sea green to deep-sea blue . . .

"The *s'ciopon* sank," Francesca was confessing to her.

"She *sank*?" That had never, Amedea let her know, been allowed to happen in her day. And in her father's certainly not.

"But we salvaged her!" Francesca protested. "It was then that Guy decided she ought to be repainted. It was, oh . . . six weeks ago. All one night it rained." She took a gulp of her wine. "And then through the next day. We kept meaning to go down to bail her out, but we forgot. It went on raining the next night. But it must have been boats chugging by too, their wakes coming on board."

"I'm sure it was," Amedea said kindly. For God forbid that one should tweak the girl's precarious self-confidence more than very, very gently. And she wanted her trust, there were things that in all decency she must try to explain to her, perhaps tonight, later . . .

"Anyway, next morning she was lying awash. Some of her floor-boards had floated away. She had plastic bags in her, a dead bird."

"But you got her up." Amedea smiled encouragingly.

"We got a rope round her thwart and dragged her as far as the bridge. It was still raining, but it was fun." Francesca was happy, remembering. She laughed. "I tied a bucket to another rope, dropped it down on its side so it filled, hauled it up. Again and again. Corrado helped – in his way. Guy kept tightening it on the rope to the thwart, raising the boat an inch at a time, making fast to the bridge. We were afraid the thwart might come away, but it didn't. After a bit the *s'ciopon* had enough freeboard for Guy to jump on board and bail."

Amedea listened to what fun it had been messing about on the bridge in the rain with ropes. She listened to how with their boat saved they had gone indoors for hot showers and coffee and croissants. She saw how then suddenly

Francesca flushed, heard her make herself finish firmly, "You would have enjoyed it."

"And our friends?" Amedea cried cheerfully. (Never would she let herself appear to feel usurped, never!) "Anthony, Claudia, everyone?"

News of Anthony Holt? He was not a man one expected to change, Francesca thought, or to do anything. His favourite restaurants and bars were still his favourite restaurants and bars – Amedea, surely, could imagine that? Quaritch still sent him their catalogues of rare books. So did Maggs. He had – wait a minute – now that she concentrated, Francesca was nearly certain – come by a fan Greta Garbo had toyed with, or was it a hat she had worn, a hat and a veil? And his ramshackle house must contain, she supposed, a few dozen more paperbacks and records than it had when Amedea had last been there – though amid such profusion how could one tell? He still on soft nights often sat in one of the squares to wait for daybreak. That was an old ritual of Guy's and his – but, of course, Amedea would know, she must have shared it with them countless times. They went dawn-watching rather like the Japanese used to go moon-watching. No, not in Piazza San Marco so much now, even at four in the morning you might see tourists. But in Campo Santo Stefano near Anthony's house. He would still go out with that candelabra of his and a bottle of wine, sometimes with a friend or two, sometimes alone, and sit at a café table in the empty square, at one of the Paolin tables, and wait for dawn. Even in Santo Stefano people passed, he grumbled; he'd have to retreat to more secret haunts. But one September night Francesca had come over Accademia bridge toward morning and seen at the end of the square his five candles shining. He had invited her to sit down with him; he had poured her a glass of wine. They had sat quietly together till the square was a bay of brackish mist shot with gold lights and rose lights – that finest Venetian hour when the water was silk and the air was muslin, and then slowly above the mist the blue came clear.

And Claudia, Amedea wanted to know, Claudia? Was she still in Venice? Ca' Zante was to be sold, she knew that. She had met Ralph Chedgrave in London – in the hands of lawyers, poor wretched man, no passport, no chequebook. (London? Francesca wondered.) Ralph had told her, using the most horrible language, that Ca' Zante was to be shut, sold.

Claudia was living alone on the top floor of the palace, Francesca said, between her bedroom and the library. A bit lonely and bored sometimes, with Nancy Goncharov dead, with Amedea away, Ralph away; and depressed because she was going to be chucked out of the house she had lived in for years, and where should she go? But she had a new lover, who was young and good-looking and showed up sometimes. Guy and Anthony and she all quite liked the lover, Francesca said. They would meet on occasion about seven in the evening in the alley by Ca' Zante carrying bottles of wine, because Claudia was so broke these days that if you wanted a drink at the palace it was a good idea to bring it with you. You had to thump on the door because the bell wouldn't ring. If you thumped loud and long, Claudia's tawny mane would appear at a high window, she'd throw the big iron key down.

A fire had broken out, had gutted one *salone* and two lesser rooms, had Amedea heard?

She had not heard. But she could believe it, she said, with that house's wiring. And the place was perhaps unlucky. The man who owned it before Ralph had been murdered in his bedroom by his boyfriend. A maid had fallen from the *altana* to the street.

Still, Francesca persisted, the palace's beleaguered

mistress entertained her friends as best she could. The record-player never had a new needle, but even scratched Monteverdi could sound pretty fine. From the windows you could watch moonlight gleam on the Grand Canal as it had always done. (Ca' Zante might be for sale, everything in it might be for sale; but it had proved a sanctuary for Guy, she wanted to declare. Claudia had done what she could, done nobly.)

Etienne Maas had bought a pair of sofas. He had come with a motorboat, they had all helped lower the sofas down the façade. Francesca herself had longed for the vast Austrian stove of painted porcelain that stood in the music room – but of course she could not afford it. Anthony Holt had bought the round table in the library. But he had left it at Ca' Zante till the very last days, so Claudia and the new lover and Guy and she should have somewhere to put their wine glasses down. And it was not half a bad library, Francesca lamented; she had found books in Italian and Latin, in English and French, bought by various owners of the house; yes, it had survived several sales; but would not outstay this one. "They're so fucking mean," Claudia had drawled to her one night, hair tossed back in disdain, one leg on the table, skirt yanked well up, "they're going to flog the fucking books." These days Francesca had almost forgotten how Claudia used to shock her.

And then the saddest day of all had come. One morning a man from Sotheby's office in Florence had knocked on the door. "You're too early!" Claudia had yelled down to the street below. The lover and she were still dallying, as the man from the auction house may have guessed, Claudia said, if he noticed that the shoulder leaned on the window was bare. "Come back in an hour, in two hours, when you please." Later the palace door was opened, the valuer was admitted, the lover expelled. "So you shouldn't put a price on him," Claudia explained. The valuer did not smile. Soon Claudia could not bear to watch him writing things down, then sticking white paper dots on the objects he had catalogued. Walking her dog to the ferry she had met Francesca, they had gone to the Lido together, tramped with the dog for miles along the shore. Claudia had dreaded going back home. She had refused categorically ever to go home again, had tramped, had called to her dog, had gone on dreading and tramping and refusing and calling. At last Francesca had persuaded her. They would go together. When they returned to Ca' Zante, she told Amedea, the white dots had spread like a disease all over the house, on furniture, on pictures, everywhere.

"And now? What will she do?"

"I think Franco Tagliapietra has offered her a bedroom in his studio. And Guy has offered her a room here. But she may go back to Ireland, she told me."

"After all these years . . ." Amedea mused. Then she smiled. "Did you know, I saw Nancy before she died? In a hospital in Padua. She was very good to me, in her way. Loyal, in her way. She –"

"Mamma!" Corrado hullooed from the foot of the stairs. "Look what I've got!"

Heaving his oar upstairs, Corrado Ashmanhaugh got the blade jammed through the balustrade. He backed it free. Turning, he clobbered the wall with the handle. He was stepping over the shaft to get a firmer grip when his mother came careering down the stairs calling Darling! Darling! He had just hit himself behind the knees with his oar and was sitting down abruptly when she was upon him, her nice smell was all about him, her softness held him, swept him off his feet, up, up, close, close, which was nice, but though he hung onto his oar for a bit as his feet left the ground then he had to let go and it fell clattering, banging, down and away.

Luckily his oar got stuck in the balustrade again, so when Mamma put him down he didn't have to go far down the stairs to reach it. Donatella was wheezing as she thudded shopping bags on to the hall bench. Francesca was coming downstairs, she helped him disentangle his oar. In the hall Mamma was kissing Papa. He said, "Let's go out on the water so Corrado can try his oar." She said, "What, the canals on a winter night?" But then luckily she said, "Well, all right. Why not?"

It had been a surprise. Papa and he had come past the Santa Fosca jetty, where the lamp in the twilight lit the church, the canal, the moored boats. They had stopped as they often did to inspect the boats upturned on the jetty, the oars propped inside the oar-maker's glowing door, the *forcola* screwed to the door which showed what work he did. Papa had said, "Wait a minute," had vanished into the workshop that even on a cold misty nightfall smelled of varnish and wood-shavings. Then Papa had come out with the old oar-maker who was carrying the oar that was to be his. Which was slighter and shorter than common oars. Which was utterly beautiful, lathed smooth, lathed true – you could run your hands along it again and again to feel the smoothness and roundedness. Which was golden, varnished shiningly. Which had been borne home proudly to the Miracoli, Papa taking one end and he the other. It had seemed a good idea to take his oar up to the *salone* to be admired there, but if they were going out in the boat it had better come downstairs again.

Corrado would be fractious by bed-time, Signora Donatella had no doubt about it. And then, helping the family get ready to go afloat (where had Amedea's winter coats been put away? could Donatella remember?) she found she had tears in her eyes, so she retreated to the kitchen. Let them go rowing. She could not bear it. She could bear nothing, suddenly.

There were her marbles in their bowl on the mantelpiece. She took a handful. But then it was hopeless, shameful; she could not hold her pretty glass spheres up to the light; could not enjoy them. She gazed at the framed photograph of Beppe and her coming out of the church arm in arm, and at the other one of him just before he went aboard that last time, and the tears trickled faster and faster down her cheeks, she could not stop them, which was wrong, very wrong, because for many years now with Our Saviour's help she had lived with her sorrow in a spirit of atonement, and having Amedea to care for had helped, and then Corrado too.

Donatella stood gripping her coloured glass globes; she ground them till they crunched. When his mother next vanished, probably the child would come out in a rash again, like he had in July.

She understood nothing about marriage, Francesca concluded – for lately the seeds of humility had been germinating in her compost brain, sometimes she could almost feel the soft, firm shoots as they slowly pushed in the enclosed, the dark, the mushy, the fertile.

She had learned nothing this year – or why did it seem, as Amedea and she put on coats, hats, scarves, as Guy and Corrado assembled oars and *forcole*, that this year had never been lived, as if it were the year before, temperate and true in its loves, innocent in its expeditions afloat?

Amedea's fingers as she shoved them into her gloves were

a bit shaky perhaps – but that just made Francesca even more giddy with bewildered compassion than before. And when on board the *s'ciopon* Amedea spilled the paraffin, wound the lantern's wick down so low it wedged, struck eight matches without lighting one, when smiling at her own incompetence she dumped the lot on the floor-boards and said, "One of you do it, please," Francesca remembered that now and then she had thought her actressy; but that had been envy of her grace, probably – contemptible; and how could you think ill of a woman because when she saw her husband and son again after four months her fingers trembled? So Francesca picked up the lantern, started trying to hoik the wick up a bit; and when Amedea smiled her gratitude she felt confided in, included, loved.

In the lighted *pietra d'Istria* archway, the rusty water-gate, heaved open, hung askew. They pushed off from the crooked mooring-posts, from the water-steps missing several blocks, glistening with slime. Black eddies sucked in the cavities in the houses' foundations. The windless, raw night was wringing; black except where a lamp or a lit window made the gloom silvery; quiet except for lappings and chucklings, a voice that called, footfalls that faded away. The tide was high, Francesca saw dark ripples slithering into a gateway, corrupting the old magnificence with their filths and salts. The seas are rising, she thought, our ruined republic will drown – but she could not feel sad (it was probably time the place went down, it had become a travesty) because Amedea was laughing as she knelt in her camel coat on the sodden grimy floor-boards and held Corrado's oar in his *forcola* for him. Guy standing in the stern, ducking as he rowed beneath the dripping hump of a bridge (his son's efforts in the bow were neither helping nor hindering much), so tall and thin in his old black oil-skin, might look like Grief himself as he sculled easily on through the murk; but he was grinning at her efforts with the stuck wick and the damp matchbox, saying "You're as cack-handed as Amedea." How could she be sad? All year (she was ashamed of her silliness, she blamed her youth) misconceptions, vaporous fears and, worst of all, vanities had been clogging in her mind like sparrows' nests in a gargoyle; but she would clean them out; because Amedea had come back, hadn't she? Here she was. Wife. Mother. Undeniable. Merry. And Guy – wise, strong man! – had forgiven, he was in control. "Look at those persimmons," he was saying as the *s'ciopon* passed a black skeletal tree miraculously bearing reddish golden fruit; "aren't they beautiful?" Perhaps his marriage was drawing the breath of resurrection right now. Yes, these sopping shadows, inhaled, were life and love. So laughing Francesca said, "I'm not left-handed like Amedea. And I'm not clumsy either. Look!" Because a match had caught; the wick, freed, wound up a centimetre, had caught. She fitted the glass cylinder back on its tin base, wound the wick down slightly now it was burning because otherwise it would smoke and the glass blacken. Corrado's oar was bumping in his *forcola*, splattering the water. The lantern's light wavered ghostlily on the boat's planking, then Francesca swung it up by its wire handle, lifted it as high as she could, and still laughing cried "Look!" again. "Look! Look!"

Because it was his birthday, and because Mamma was back, (his conscious mind had nearly forgotten she had been away), Corrado was allowed to have everybody come to his bedroom to listen to his story with him. His story was meant to be *The Pied Piper of Hamelin*, but it kept becoming an Indian story because he liked Indian stories best of all, and his father was obliging about transforming stories that were insufficiently Indian, letting them wander east. So tonight Guy explained how when he was a boy in the Nilgiri Hills, on certain evenings there was music at the temple nearby. The music came from the temple across some scrub and tussocks where water-buffaloes grazed and were sleeping now. Corrado wriggled with pleasure in his bed-clothes. Guy recounted how the music drifted through the garden trees, then through the hibiscus on the veranda, through the chick-blinds of his bedroom. He got it muddled up with the Pied Piper fifing in Hamelin, he said, because this music too, stealing in from the Indian night to enrapture a European child, promised an undiscovered country. This enchanter might have played the rats away, come back now for the boys and girls. He had always wished he had had the courage to creep away to the temple, Guy confessed. Did Corrado not agree that wherever it was the Pied Piper led the children, it was probably a lot more interesting than Hamelin?

Trooping down from Corrado's room, Signora Donatella (who was sure that if the child had not turned fractious this evening, he was bound to tomorrow) said she would not have dinner with them. No, no, thank you, truly not. She would eat an omelette in the kitchen; she would go early to bed. "Welcome home," she said to Amedea, and kissed her good night.

Francesca flushed. She havered. Oh God, had she been obtuse *again*? *Of course* Guy and Amedea would want to dine alone together. But they protested, "Don't you dare bolt!" and ordered, "Don't be an idiot. Sit down, shut up."

Had they remembered hyacinth bulbs? Amedea wanted to know, abandoning her knife and fork after three mouthfuls of grilled bass, sipping her wine. When they had been potted, they should be set in a dark cupboard. Oh, all the autumn things . . . What about *moeche*, those small crabs that when they change their shells are so light they float to the surface so the fishermen can skim them up easily? *Moeche* so soft you eat them whole, crunching, snapping, claws and all – had they got Corrado to like them? And what about the *vin novo* this year? Had they been to the Milion or the Do Mori to drink the new wine that is still fermenting when it is siphoned into your glass? And, come to think of it, this autumn had the man from the boatmen's watering-hole round the corner asked for some pomegranates from the garden tree when they were ripe? Every year since she could remember he had come, he had cut some of the – "What colour would you say they are, Guy? Francesca? not vermilion, not scarlet exactly" – some of the pomegranates, because with sprigs of their green leaves they looked decorative hung on the café wall along with the football calendar and the crucifix.

Francesca listened happily. (If she had let the gargoyle she bore on her drainpipe neck get clogged with rotting sparrows' nests, at least this evening she was sensibly clearing them out.) Now Guy was telling how he had paid his annual visit to Clive Mellis. Did Amedea remember the damp cottage out on the littoral at San Nicolò where the old poet lived with his young wife, their small children? Of course she remembered! Always chicken for lunch. Rooms full of books growing mould. One did not forget. The fishermen in the courtyard who when they were sober mended the children's bicycles. The monks who walked across from their cloister to discuss Ariosto. She wondered – had Guy and Clive strolled that way? – was there still a recruit dreaming his youth away (and really that was a stupid waste, a disgrace!) guarding the overgrown track into the woods of the military camp? And the old fellow who lived in that even more tumble-down cottage in the elder thicket behind the hamlet, the old fellow who used to breed pouter pigeons – was he still alive?

Francesca finished her bass, her potatoes roasted with rosemary, her artichoke hearts, and listened tranquilly. It was obvious, Amedea must observe it too, how unchanging Guy Ashmanhaugh was. He had urged the man from the bar to cut as many pomegranates as he wanted. To contemplate a design on a drawing-board he still stood as he had always stood, slightly stooped, his brown forelock flopping, left hand clasping his right elbow, right hand at his chin. This autumn as every autumn his cotton and linen had given way to tweed and corduroy. On hands and knees beside Corrado on a rug, with pencil and paper he had taught him to distinguish Doric, Ionic, Corinthian; the boy was beginning to draw them. Especially now that his faithless wife, deciding that she could not be bothered with the *pecorino*, lighting a cigarette, had started to talk about Tuscany in what seemed to Francesca the most enviably grown-up manner, with openness but with tact . . . Now that Guy was listening apparently without emotion . . . Was it not clear that for steadfastness and magnanimity he had not his like in all Europe? And must not Amedea recognise this, love this? Francesca Ziani had no fear of ever being an unfaithful wife. But she had no doubts either that her future husband must resemble her cousin's in every respect.

Above Il Cerreto stretched woods of sweet chestnut, higher again the Appenines were bare sheep-walk. Under blue skies Gérard Charry and Amedea Lezze had walked for miles. All you heard were sheep-bells coming and going on the breeze, the voices of larks high over the heather and bilberries. Buzzards soared. Once they met a man and his family who had been collecting the ripe bilberries, they were carrying them down the mountain in trugs, their hands and the trugs stained blue. Never anyone else. The streams' banks were pocked by sheep. In the swamps, iris and rush grew, and mosses of green after green after green. Butterflies flitted up under your feet. Once they had come to a small lake, they had swum, lain afterward drying on warm stones. (At this Guy smiled with his eyes, not just with his mouth, Francesca noticed with awe, as if he were sincerely happy for the lovers' happiness.) Then back in the car down rocky tracks that after rain were water-courses, chunks of limestone spattering sideways from the wheels. Lower down, softer tracks, a forester's stone house here and there, boulders on its roof against gales. Once they had found a charcoal burner's hut and smoking mound. Signs of copsing on some hillsides, wood felled and stacked, tractor tyres in the mud. Sometimes a church bell clanked, otherwise what villages there were lay quiet, a few grey houses bunched around a stocky church, a stocky tower.

Listening, Francesca saw Il Cerreto standing four-square among its clumps of oak trees; saw the honey-coloured plaster and the grey stone, the straggle of lesser buildings; how below the terrace the land fell away, vineyards turning russet, a peach orchard from which the fruit had been picked, spinneys of cypress and oak, hay fields gone to clover, the valley of tilted patches of changing browns and greens. Apparently there was a *fienile*: one of those Tuscan haysheds, Amedea explained to her provincial cousin who had never gone far afield from the Mestre outskirts and the Venetian lagoon, with brick lattices instead of windows to let the air blow through but keep the rain out. The chapel, Francesca saw, with its graveyard. She imagined Gérard and Amedea lazing away their mornings in deck-chairs under the umbrella pine; bees in the lavender, the veronica – all the live murmur of a summer's day; smell of box parterre when the sun got at it. Then at evening, mist in the valley, owls' cries. And indoors Gérard the acknowledged lover of the lady of the house (but not quite the master, was that right? though that might have come), the lighter of fires, opener of bottles of wine. Francesca tried to imagine how much or how little they had entertained. But it was impossible to be sure, because the friends Amedea mentioned – Luca Baldeschi and his wife Angelica for instance – were all by ill luck among those immortals of Amedea's pantheon that her prosaic cousin, because she had never seen them incarnate, had trouble believing in.

Between waking and sleeping, Corrado was riding a water-buffalo. In her bedroom, Signora Donatella – who knew that to break faith is always and only immoral, that such evil will spawn only suffering, ever more suffering, until it is redeemed by Our Lord's blood – was on her knees. At the dining table, Guy Ashmanhaugh – whose head ached; who knew it must be possible to go through the motions of family life even in despair if one's wife required it of one, but had not conceived it could be quite this horrible; who hoped for no better than this mockery, and feared worse – crossed his legs, lit a cigar.

Sitting beside him, Francesca imagined Gérard alone at Il Cerreto and judged it brilliant the way Amedea, while chatting about peach orchards, let her listeners grasp that her Tuscan love affair had not been as perfect as all that, had begun to come to pieces almost at once, one might deduce, for it seemed she had been away elsewhere fairly often, and usually elsewhere alone. Better than brilliant, Francesca corrected herself: kind. But poor Gérard! (Where was he now?) Amedea was still talking about the countryside. And Francesca saw Gérard walking alone through the fields and woods after rain, hearing rivulets all around. Walking for miles, trying not to be unhappy – what else had he got to do? Probably after a downpour like that – Francesca brought to mind the drenching gusts, the vexed trees – hardly anyone went out to the glistening olive groves, or to the vineyards which now the vintage was past were only posts, wires, lopped stubs. Yes, probably Gérard didn't see a soul. Just skylines of cypress and umbrella pine receding back hill after hill in the blowing, bright evening air. Francesca saw the walker trudge along a boggy path by the rim of a pond where gusts were heaving the dying sedge about; where the last water-lilies of the year were flapped up, then flopped down again. Poor sad Gérard! Was it hypocritical to be sorry for both the men in love with her cousin? Anyhow, there Francesca saw Gérard stand, shielding his eyes to gaze at the ripples that blazed silver in the westering sun, chestnut leaves whirling past his eyes, past dead weed drifting down-wind and a fish that jumped. Then naturally he'd come back to Venice; term had started;

he'd gone sculling on his own . . . What was Amedea saying? Francesca forgot Gérard.

What else had she been up to? Amedea was vague. Oh, she'd gone to stay with Valeria Maris, and she'd . . .

Well in fact, if they really wanted to know, she'd been visiting art galleries. Getting on and off aeroplanes, checking into hotels and checking out, eating on her own in restaurants – and going to art galleries and museums. Because . . . They'd laugh at her when they heard . . . Her father – Francesca probably only remembered him very faintly – her father had once explained the theory of heaven to her like this. Heaven was all the great Venetian paintings, he had said. But some had been lost in fires or otherwise destroyed, and many had been dispersed around the world. The surviving pieces of the Venetian heaven were hopelessly scattered, and we couldn't ransom them.

So, his daughter declared and laughed, she'd had the idea of fitting a few of the bits together. Not knowing what to do with herself, she'd begun to do that. She had been to Dresden, had stood before Giorgione's *Venere dormiente*. She had visited Paris for the pictures the French had stolen, London for a ceiling from Ca' Contarini. Her father had had some odd ideas – but this notion of his about heaven had come back to her – did Guy and Francesca understand it at all? – and she rather liked it. Not a seat of judgement and of justice, her father's kingdom of God. Come to that, not a kingdom. A marine republic, no? Anyway, just hues, lines, shimmerings of a lost dignity and loveliness one could try to piece together in one's head. And dead right too – Amedea lifted a candle-stick, lit another cigarette – for how could mankind's virtues and vices merit appraisal at the gate of a heaven worth imagining?

Francesca had scarcely been listening. Her heart was squalling like a baby, it was dreadful, why wouldn't it stop? God, God, she should *never* have foisted herself on Guy. As soon as her cousin left, she should have looked for other lodgings. Ah *why* hadn't she thought? She should never have let herself mother Corrado. She blushed. Right now she would make amends. Right now. She would leave them to talk. She would go to bed.

Guy stood up. He said his head was aching. He said good night.

The other side of the city Ralph Chedgrave, an outlaw put ashore in Italy from a friend's yacht, found the locks at Ca' Zante had been changed. Well, never mind, he would borrow Nancy's gardener's ladder, use it to climb his own old garden wall. Or at least he would sit with Nancy and have a drink and talk about the old days. He walked down the alley to her gate. But her house, like his own, was silent, dark.

He came back, stood on the bridge parapet, managed to scramble over the wall into the Ca' Zante garden. After a confused attempt to break in through a window, he tried to climb back over the wall, but it stood higher on the inside. He tried to scrabble up the ivy, but it came away, he fell back. No trees stood against the wall, damn it . . . ah, but the fountain did. He stood on the fountain, but his arms wouldn't lift him any higher. The marble was slimy, he fell. In his tweed suit, he lay down on the wet leaves.

"Do you want me to go?" Francesca had knitted her fingers. "I think I ought to go. Oh God, I'm sorry I stayed. I just didn't *think*."

Here's your chance, Amedea had exhorted herself. You may be the soul of dishonour – you are the soul of dishonour – but you can treat your young cousin decently this time. Treat her fairly. Just for a change.

"No, I certainly don't want you to go. You must choose what you do. But . . . I don't want you to feel trapped – do you understand?" Amedea had asked as softly, gently as she knew how. "Of course it'll be wonderful for Guy and Corrado if you stay. But they'd be all right without you." She had smiled. "Less all right than with you. But all right."

Christ! the voice of evil – no, the voice of understanding – had snarled in Amedea's head: Can't I even behave honourably without being guilty of trying to be liked? (*Again* I've misunderstood everything, Francesca's heart had sobbed with frustration. But then with dignity, with happy abnegation she had declared to herself how she would stay beside Guy whose wife did not love him, who would visit him but never love him again, with Guy whose head ached, who rowing in a black oilskin on a November night was Grief himself. She would stay with Signora Donatella who coughed rackingly, whose prayers were never answered. With Corrado, Strassa, the child's oar propped against that pilaster.) *God Almighty!* Amedea's jackal voice had sneered: Exhausted? A modicum of virtue – nothing spectacular – a little doing of the decent thing – to leave Guy and Corrado together in peace – to point out to Francesca that she doesn't *have* to sacrifice herself – and I can barely lift my coffee cup for weariness. She lived in Venice and rowed on the lagoon – Amedea had begun to tell the story of herself because if she didn't she wouldn't exist any more, with that hopelessness she had been sure she wouldn't. So . . . Odds. Ends. A husband who read Bergson in bed. And then a love – just ennui and desire probably, she must remember not to glorify things – but it had often seemed that she knew she was bearing it. Still seemed like that sometimes. Not now, if she were honest. But . . . Sometimes her love was embedded in her mind like the old fable says toads have a jewel in their heads. However, not now.

It would be so easy to put some Vivaldi on the record-player, so pleasant to dream. But no. Because there were things she wanted to get straight, things she ought to try to put squarely before Francesca. (It might be weeks, might be months before they found themselves sitting alone together again like this in front of the *salone* fireplace. And sooner or later Francesca would have to resolve this and resolve that.) Perhaps if she started with simple things . . .

Gérard liked introducing her to his neighbours, Amedea told Francesca and smiled. In the rowing club along the Misericordia. In the eating-house along the Ormesini where the signora always heaped extra dollops of *seppie* on his *polenta*, grilled him the fattest *cefalo* or *bosega*; where when they tied up the *sandolo* her husband insisted they carry their oars, *forcole* and lantern inside so they should not be stolen; where the tables had brass corners; where a brown canvas awning swagged in the doorway, people lifted it aside when they came in from the quay.

Amedea liked most of Gérard's neighbours. The carpenter, for example . . . Although once, it had been unfortunate, when she had arrived at the Misericordia in the *sandolo* he had borrowed her oar so that he could join in the beating to death of a *pantegana*, one of the ancient and grand lagoon rats. They were nearly extinct, though lesser rats endured multitudinously, and the pleasure of the rare chase was such that the carpenter had not wished to waste time by stepping into his workshop for a pole. The *pantegana* was swimming in circles because one of the men clubbing the canal with oars had dislocated its back; this made the hunt simpler. Some of the men stood on the quay to flail, others stood in boats. Amedea moored the *sandolo*. Gérard heard the shouts and the splashing, he came out. They watched the killing a bit ruefully, Amedea waiting to be given her oar back. It took several minutes for the men to break enough bones for the rat to drown.

There was the plumber too, Amedea recounted. (But would she have the guts to tell Francesca how she had let Gérard dream they might live in Tuscany indefinitely; had let him give up his job, apply to the Tuscan universities; had gone to Spain without him, to the Prado to look at Venetian pictures; had let him come back to Venice where someone else now had his job, where he was scratching a living with translations?) There was the plumber who only had space for one customer at a time in his shop, on account of the basins, the lavatories, the wreaths of taps on bindertwine. He had a photograph of his wife in the drawer of washers. He had not spoken to her since her infidelity during the war, though she lived around the corner. Once he had insisted that Amedea squeeze in among the taps so she too could be shown the betrayer in her lost youth and loveliness. The plumber also had another room behind; but it had not been cleared up since the flood of 1966. The air was foetid; slime covered the floor, the walls. It was jumbled with the wreckage of the radios and sewing-machines his brother the electrician had been going to sell before that tide reached the ceiling.

In Tuscany, the caretaker at Il Cerreto let his spaniel out into the garden to cock its leg. Moonlight glistened on the orange trees. The Venetian lady and her so-called husband had kept the lease of the place, but they'd disappeared. (Those two weren't married – his wife had been positive about that; they were nice, but they weren't married; she could tell.) At Christmas they might come, they had said. Christmas and the New Year, possibly. And in the spring, yes, of course! Where had that dog got to? It must have cocked its leg by now. He whistled.

Off the Venetian coast, birds clogged in an oil slick. By the light of the moon, a dolphin with its lungs clogged with oil seemed to emboss the black water. Clogged eels were twists and frays of silver.

On the Grand Canal at the Casinò Municipale, Luca Baldeschi (one of Amedea Lezze's friends who *did* exist) strolled away from the roulette table where his wife was losing, her smile coming and going under the chandelier. Squared black shoulders of men. Rounded white shoulders of women. To stop himself yawning, Baldeschi lit a cigarette.

In the house at the Miracoli, Francesca Ziani's blood had stopped gallivanting through her heart; it was walking. So – next spring Corrado and she would be back in the squares. But would she ever have a child of her own?

"Nancy!" Amedea sprang to her feet, went to the sideboard, poured two glasses of brandy. "I got interrupted, I never told you how . . ."

She had perched on the side of Nancy Goncharov's hospital bed. Travel was what the dying woman had suggested. By the way, had Francesca noticed how Venice's old ladies were thinning out? A pity. The place had had rather a good array of old ladies. Nancy dead. And the old Queen of Yugoslavia had vanished, had been tucked away somewhere discreet where she could come to grief in peace. Who else? Oh yes, Cristina Montalba had just died – they used to call her Venice's one-woman jet-set. And Tania Aldridge too. Had Francesca ever met Tania? She had lived the first twenty years of her life in Russia, the second twenty in China, the third in the United States – that was where she had come by her last surname – and the fourth here.

Nancy was the only one Amedea had introduced her to, Francesca said.

Ah, really, was that so? Well anyway, Nancy had suggested travel. She had understood her need for impermanence – after living in one house all her life, after marriage, motherhood – and she had suggested – could Francesca guess? it was too ridiculous – the Levant! Gérard and she should light out to the Lebanon, if they felt like keeping on changing their minds. Of course when she spoke English she had talked about the Lebanon, in her old-fashioned way. The Sudan too. The Argentine. A blank my mind went, Amedea recalled. The Near East . . . ? That was where those three upstart monotheisms had come from wasn't it? she had protested. And where the brutes of all three dogmas were still slugging it out. Why should Nancy think a pagan like her might want to go there? But the old lady propped up on hospital pillows had said it was paradise in her day. Lemon groves along the sea. And one could speak French. And the fish restaurants of Beirut, and the dancing – oh la la! Amedea laughed, she sipped. You've forgotten the fighting there, she had told her father's old friend. Ah, Nancy had conceded, perhaps things might not be quite so brilliant as they had been; but Amedea must remember to disregard the kind of people who took any notice of religion or race. Yes, Nancy, she had protested, but . . . No buts, she had been told. If they act from considerations of faith or blood, give them no weight. Adamant, Nancy had been. Then she had gone back to describing the dancing on Beirut nights. She had laughed; had said, "When I was alive . . ."

And it wasn't only the need for impermanence that Nancy Goncharov had understood. (Amedea stepped over her son's anchored fleet, reached the French windows, turned on her heel, paced back on her sentry-go.) The need to give away, too. Did Francesca know what she meant? (Truly it was beyond endurance, the schoolgirlishness with which she sat in that chair.) The need, sometimes, to render up. She herself hardly knew what she meant. Often she thought she would die of half understanding things. That, one day, would be her particular brain tumour. But – she had been right, she thought, to give her house to Guy; and right to renounce her child. Oh, she knew what the world thought. But she didn't agree with the world. Excellent brandy, wasn't it? Would Francesca like some more? No? Then she would help herself. Yes, sometimes to renounce could seem a more – a more what? – a more acute form of love than to possess. But to hell with that. Bullshit, probably. Or conceivably not . . . Had Francesca seen a painting – it was in Paris – she'd been hunting for Venetian stuff and had wandered into the wrong gallery – a painting of a prince called Sardanapalus on his death-bed? Good embroidered death-bed. Sardanapalus was watching his Arab horses and his concubines being killed. Making sure no one else would enjoy them. Standard conduct, she dared say, among despots. But also, just possibly, he'd been divesting his soul of the love of created things. It didn't matter if Francesca hadn't seen the painting. The point was, she sometimes felt the same longing, and what was more she gave herself the credit for satisfying it a bit more decently than Sardanapalus did. For yes – Francesca would have guessed – one of these fine days she was going to have to divest her soul of the love of Gérard Charry – or her soul would divest itself and her conscience claim the credit. Because it was too exhausting, going from one cliché to another – first the English husband, then the French lover – going from Venice to Tuscany to everywhere – oh she didn't know. But sometimes she felt like a hermit crab. Francesca must know those poor naked little crabs that decamped from empty shell to empty shell. Well, she crawled from idea to idea and feeling to feeling a bit like that. It was lucky, was it not, that the dead left their concepts, their carapaces, their conventions, their clichés, ah God help her, lying about on our shores? Lucky, that is, if you didn't happen, yourself, to grow a shell. So she crawled.

Out of the last ill-adapted shell. On, soft, ugly, vulnerable across the sand. Praying there'd be another vacant shell lying about somewhere. Praying the gulls screaming overhead didn't see her and swoop down with their shadows and stab.

A bit like Diogenese, Francesca suggested. What might Diogenese have had in his head, she wondered, if he'd ever crawled out of his barrel and set off in search of another one? And she stood up – because it was terrible to sit and watch Amedea fret to and fro, hear her talk herself to pieces lightly, harshly. She wanted to distract her; she wanted to comfort her. (This was new, she suddenly realised. She had never felt this toward her cousin before.)

But Amedea did not wish to be approached. Not yet. She went on with her sentry-go. Like Diogenese . . . ? She supposed vaguely like Diogenese. Very vaguely. Anyhow, the old fellow had stayed in his tub, hadn't he? No, she was more like a reel of masking tape, the way she stuck wound up. In Tuscany she had tried to unwind, had tried and tried. But it had been hard – what with missing Corrado – feeling guilty that she didn't miss him more – remembering what the world thought of women who left their children. And then of course she had behaved vilely. Amedea took a gulp of brandy. Behaved vilely to Gérard. Would Francesca care for a gruesome detail or two? Well, one night after dinner on the terrace he had asked her – had asked her as he sat there matter-of-factly cutting up a nectarine – Would she like them, one day, to have a child? And could Francesca guess the foul answer she'd given him? (She could not. In agitation, in pity, she shook her head. She recalled Gérard at an earlier dinner table, peeling an orange.) She had said that she was spending so much money on him, she didn't think she could afford another nanny right then.

Not that Gérard was to be sorrowed for too profusely. (Gérard who had lost his heart to her – would never marry – would drift distractedly on through life – never make any money.) Amedea shrugged her shoulders, she waved her cigarette. He'd been a fool to suggest such a thing – he who knew how happy she was to take her pill each evening, sow that one white seed. He, of all people, should have known better. (Gérard Charry who with his well-sculpted profile and his poetry in the literary journals was the kind of young man that fashionable women have always doted on – the jackal voice knew all about it.) Hadn't that supposed miracle of his been all about the delight of living in the beginnings of dissolution? Then who the hell was he to dream they might live as man and wife at Il Cerreto or anywhere else, to dream of children, to dream that the frailties of passionate love might survive among the shadows of the solidities of domestic contentment? (Gérard who in years to come in Tuscany would have taken to wearing cardigans – bitch! hypocrite! she railed, I dreamed too! of course I did, I longed! – and drinking gin and French and writing about the Sienese school.) Indeed, it had been that miracle of his that had started her thinking a love affair with him might be possible. Not just desirable. Possible. Yes, she knew she'd behaved treacherously toward Francesca back in the spring. Did saying you were sorry do any good? She was, she guessed, trying to make amends in her way. Anyhow, Gérard had gone white. He had said he hadn't thought they need employ a nanny. She had said she hadn't meant it. Oh, Francesca could imagine.

Could Francesca imagine? Amedea Lezze had her doubts. But she couldn't spell out *everything* for the girl. Couldn't explain, for instance, how that night she had pitched all her ardour and imagination and sweetness into making love. She laughed, she stubbed out her cigarette. The sexual enslavement, of course, remained; the fates were just, merciful.

But one thing she would try to say. One thing. Would Francesca please have patience another minute or two? Then, she promised, she would be quiet. Yes, yes, she would stop marching up and down too. Stop this trudging from rug to rug – it was funny, had Francesca thought of it? – from Shiraz to Bokhara to Tashkent – her father had bought them here and there. But this she wanted to say. This. If there had been a failure in Tuscany it had been a different one. All to do with how Gérard loved the smell of cypress trees. No, she hadn't gone mad. This was the essence, Francesca must please believe her, this was the one vital thing. They had been walking along the drive at Il Cerreto. It was a long enfilade of cypress shade. And Gérard had wanted to know: Was the resinous scent suffusing her mind with peace too? (A hare had cantered off through the peach orchard.) After a mind radiant with Venetian lagoon light, was a mind pungent with Tuscan cypress an equal happiness? They had strolled past the pond (a grass snake had swum away) and she had remembered how she had longed for a love – she supposed it was love, the very highest – had longed for a feeling, perhaps nothing more than that . . . But . . . As if by grace the same blood could suffuse two grey minds with one flush of rose. Yes, that had been it. And then they had come upon the gardener, who had done some copsing and was chucking cypress saplings on to his bonfire. And suddenly with that resinous burning in the air Gérard had declared that his mind had become a silver censer of smoking cypress chips swung from the hand of an angelic gardener, and he had wanted to know immediately, had demanded excitedly, Did she feel anything equivalently crazy? And the sad thing was, she had not.

Amedea sat down on the marquetry chair. She leaned her head back against the cool looking-glass.

Along Fondamenta della Misericordia, Gérard Charry was walking home. The perfect balance that he had imagined between Amedea and him was awry, he knew it. His pan of the scales was weighed down with hopeless love. The other was tipped high, where for a moment she'd alight and then dance up again . . .

Ah to hell with it. And at least he'd been right about one thing. That Dead Sea scroll laid up in her breast, that prophecy, that writing, what-have-you. It was her sheer conventionality that had given her away. Hidden in the disappointed wife and the wearied, amateurish mother and the socialite was the enormous, simple hope of an abstract love – a faith just as conventional as everything else about her, just as unimaginative . . . Why couldn't he stop nagging at his image of her?

In the belfry of San Marziale, the bells were still hanged by their heels like gigantic bronze bats waiting to kick into flight. On the Servi wall, the statue of the Madonna still stood under her tin canopy. Once on that quay Gérard had felt the whole world die every instant in his head, then with each pulse momently a new world come alive. Once his shoes on the flagstones had been the triumphant tempo of time consigning all good and evil, all truth and falsity, to the beginning of their decay. But now his plodding feet sounded like fish slapped on a slab.

Feebly Amedea Lezze tried to start the story of herself. Her father taking her to look at a Tiepolo ceiling, smiling up at that cracked entablature, those chariot wheels, those banners, those clouds, those girls' white legs swung from billowing silks, tugging his moustaches, saying, "That's heaven up there. Attractive." Her husband who took

Nietzsche on picnics. Her son . . . But Francesca was burbling something. What?

They had been at Pellestrina, Guy and she. (Francesca wanted to lay before Amedea the best thing she was, the truest thing she knew. And now she was clear about what that was, and she was sure Amedea would understand.) They had watched the sun playing off the lagoon on the red and yellow and blue houses. They had watched the day fishermen come ashore, land their catch, roll up their nets. By the time the night fishermen were putting forth, Guy and she had taken the ferry one littoral nearer Venice. They had strolled along the sea-wall, birds twittering in the sedge – Amedea knew what it was like. Dusk on the sea to one's right. Dusk on the lagoon to one's left. But then Guy had stopped. He had pointed ahead to Malamocco church tower, to the island of Poveglia far off. He had said he didn't know why, but . . . When he came this way he always saw Dürer's *Melencolia*. Had she ever seen that engraving? he had wondered. She had said yes.

Amedea had been trying to cheer herself up by deciding that if she ever went to heaven she'd go in that Poiret gown of her grandmother's. No one should compare with her for fallal. But now she lifted her short black hair from the looking-glass.

She had listened to Guy describing what he saw, Francesca said. Bats flittering. The winged woman sitting in despair. A skinny lurcher asleep. And indeed there had been bats in the air, a dog in a yard. Then Guy had talked about all the clutter that came with the angel. A sphere, an hour-glass, compasses, a rainbow, what else? Francesca couldn't remember now. Oh yes, a comet, a *putto*, carpenters' tools. And then, while she had still been bewildered, he had asked her – Could she see it?

In heaven Amedea would have her state rooms by Sansovino, her bacchanalia by Poussin, her solitudes by Leopardi – but why must this silly little bitch (what a waste of time, trying to explain things to her! and now she was exhausted) stand here bragging about Guy being nice to her, and about whatever this angel was?

Of course she could *imagine* the angel, Francesca explained. "Just like you could *imagine* Gérard's angelic gardener." But to think with Guy's thought, see with his sight . . . ? She had shaken her head. He had laughed. She was probably right, he had said, and the angel wasn't there. But she might be. Or she might have been there once. Dürer had been in Venice, apparently, a few years before he made that engraving.

But how stupid of her! she exclaimed, to go chattering about things Amedea must know far more about. (Amedea's silence was unsettling. Francesca twined her fingers.) It was only that – only that Guy's angel was unforgettable, there on the shore at nightfall – and he had wanted to give it to her – and now she had wanted to give it back. "Give it to you!" Francesca insisted nervously. "Didn't Gérard want your head to be a smoking censer like his? And then you told me about that. And then I thought: I know what we share. The angel. The impossibility of seeing the angel."

"Ah . . . !" Amedea smiled. "That old angel of Guy's."

Four

The first time that Gérard Charry realised how imprisoned Amedea felt it was still winter.

Day broke. She got out of bed, began to dress – she had a flight to catch, she was going to Amsterdam to look at pictures. She glanced out of his attic window. "Christ! How often does that *squero* flood?"

Of course they had heard the warning sirens. But they'd imagined the usual *acqua alta*, nothing much, ripples ankle-deep on the quays. Gérard went downstairs to have a look. The bottom five steps were underwater. Back upstairs in his flat he found Amedea frenziedly telephoning taxi-boat companies, trying to bully them into sending vessels that were already busy, hectoring, wheedling. She cracked the telephone down. "Get me out of here! Where's that boat of yours I had built?"

Gérard explained that he'd never get to Rio dell'Avogaria and back in time. If she wanted to be on that aeroplane, she'd have to wade. He would carry her suitcase.

As soon as she knew she wasn't treed in his mansard she cheered up, he noticed. She'd be out of the country in a few hours, she was blithe, she splashed along beside him. She was up to her waist, she was ruining her clothes, she'd have to change at the airport. But when people at windows called and laughed, she, floundering along, called back, laughed too. At Piazzale Roma she promised the taxi-driver she'd pay him double for wetting his car seat.

When spring came, they got to work refitting *Zenobia*. Amedea would talk happily about the voyage they would make; she seemed more calm; would saunter with Gérard to Sant'Alvise on a still evening and watch the boys diving into the canal. Of course they weren't meant to, and of course they did, she would say mildly. She would stroll with him into the garden at the Groggia; and admire the yews and the holm oaks and the palms; and discuss the restoration of the villa; and lament a dying magnolia. And she would always row about Cannaregio with him. It was enough to suggest the notion in the vaguest terms. Yes, yes! She would be ready in ten minutes, in five! One day it was raining – soft May rain. They put on oilskins; they took an oar each; they took a bottle of champagne; they rowed. (Francesca Ziani, crossing a bridge with her umbrella, saw them. The boat was drifting – they were laughing – standing in the rain in their drifting boat – passing each other the champagne and laughing at something. Francesca's stomach fluttered, her cheeks flushed. Let them not have seen me! she prayed, angling her umbrella between them and her, hurrying on.)

Then Amedea became excited because one day when she was in the archive at the Frari, leafing through old maps, she found a plan which, she announced, made Venice look like a diagram of the skull. A skull and all the bits and pieces in it, the works. Venice breathed through the Grand Canal. The Giudecca Canal was for food. Gérard could see, couldn't he? And wasn't it splendid that her city was a mind? She didn't suppose that much thinking went on in the poor old head any more. But he must come with her, they were going to visit the broken nose, up where the church of Corpus Domini used to stand. And they went. She led him stumbling over railway sidings. Then he must come with her again, they would take the *sandolo*, because although the head had been chopped off there were chunks of the neck floating dotted about – the island of La Grazia, for instance, which had once had a church too, had he ever landed there?

But Amedea was most peaceful when she was down at the marina working on her yacht. She liked it the day they reeved a new spinnaker halyard, because when Gérard spliced the new halyard to the old one and hoisted it up it jammed in the sheave (his splice was too clumsy, too thick! she mocked him) so they had to rig a makeshift bosun's chair, and she could insist it was her who was hauled up the old wooden mast. Gérard stood on the cutter's deck, he winched steadily, his lover ascended. At the masthead she jabbed into the sheave with her marline spike, she freed the splice – and then just stayed up there, didn't want to come down, hung aloft like a flag on a windless day, looking out to the islands, letting the lagoon lap, the light lap.

Then at evening it was peaceful to row ashore in *Zenobia*'s tender, to walk through the alleys of Castello where voices called from house to house over their heads. Gulls scavenged in canals, children skirmished in *campielli*.

When the hot weather came, at night along the Misericordia and the Ormesini there were often skiffs with lanterns passing or mooring or casting off. It was a cranny of Venice so tranquil, where life was changing so gradually that people still took kitchen chairs out by the water as they did in the lagoon villages. So when it was too sweaty to sleep early, Gérard's neighbours gathered, grandparents, babies, everyone. Gérard and Amedea would lean against the wall that would still be warm because it faced south and the sun had beaten all day. Or they would climb to his attic where the windows were never closed, they would lean on a sill. Quiet voices washed over the water, bumped off the masonry. When there were no more rowers to watch, they watched the moored craft, the way their lamplit reflections steadied and came clear. When everyone else had gone to sleep, all they heard were the nudging of gunwhales against posts.

That was a good hour to put out in the *sandolo*, go gliding through the shadows of bridges, drift to a standstill on glassy reaches. Sometimes they were still out on the canals when at sea the sun, rising, floated gut uppermost like a leviathan which, dead, spilled its fiery giblets, lights, chitterlings, fed all the worms in the sea. Had Gérard and Amedea already been sailing to Greece, they would have seen the sun's innards deliquescing over miles of wrinkled grey. But as they were on the Grand Canal what they saw was Gérard's old friend the water-skiing goddess of daybreak who, he told his lover, jumped the raked Lido, planked her skis down on the lagoon, skied swishing into town behind a speedboat of roseate spindrift, swished ashore at for example San Marcuola because that was where the *sandolo* happened to be drifting that sunrise, kicked off her skis . . .

All these things we do together, Gérard thought. Only it is a pity Amedea does not care to share with me her flights to Leningrad and to Geneva. It is a pity also that I have to keep reminding myself that when she talks admiringly of Carl This and Stefano That and Yves The Other it is because with me she desires all the uncertainty of a love affair. And there are other things that it is not to her taste that we should share. Rainy spring afternoons when you dodge through the shambling columns of tourists to deliver a translation of great dullness you sat up half the night to complete, and a tourist's umbrella jabs your eye and you notice a Judas tree in full blood and the work is paid meanly and late.

A couple of days before *Zenobia* sailed, Anthony Holt gave a party in the courtyard behind his house. The families from the other houses which backed on to the yard all came; they brought cakes and bottles; they brought nephews, nieces, cousins. It was a good party, with trestle tables, with Japanese lanterns. Everybody was enjoying it, until Amedea Lezze, drunk, decided a tall Austrian girl was too attractive to Gérard Charry, or not beautiful enough for him, it was difficult to tell what she had decided, she kept spitting different things.

Next day she went back to apologise. Gérard went with her. They found Francesca Ziani helping to clear up. It was raining. Anthony gave them lunch in his kitchen. Through the open door, they watched the downpour battering the courtyard weeds. It smelled fresh.

The day was sad, because Anthony had just been telephoned by Claudia Glaven in London. Ralph Chedgrave had fallen down a staircase, he had had a haemorrhage, he was dead. That and the wine at lunch added to the wine of the night before made Amedea tremulous. Did Anthony know that, when Guy had visited India the month before, she had gone back to the Miracoli? To be with Corrado. She had begged Guy not to take the boy. No, no, she was a liar, she had not begged, she had merely asked, of course. And of course Guy had not demurred; had visited his mother alone. So she could be with Corrado . . . That had been the idea. In fact she had scuttled round in her usual scatty circles, she confessed, Anthony could ask Gérard or Francesca, they knew, half the days she had been out of Venice, half the nights at the Misericordia. He was going to open another bottle of the Malbec, wasn't he? Oh, well, never mind. If it was finished, that Refosco would do fine.

Anthony said he was glad Corrado had seen more of her. But why, he mused, was his dearest Amedea (to whom he could scarcely refuse wine if she asked for it, and anyway presumably she would retreat to bed this afternoon?)

drumming up such a rataplan about Corrado? Unreconstructed patrician that she was, she'd never had any doubt, so far as Anthony had observed, that she would be a more amusing mama if a lot of the daily upbringing of the child were entrusted to his nanny. And Corrado, his godfather had thought when he recently came to tea, was fine. There had been the danger, last year, that Amedea and Gérard, eloped to Tuscany, might stay there. But that danger had passed. Doubtless the love affair would pass; and Corrado would still be only a child; and Guy and Amedea would still be firmer friends than a lot of married couples Anthony could think of. Unmarried, he temperately approved of the good sense of matrimony. A marriage endured. It could accommodate and forgive a few passions. People let one another be. It was sad, of course, for dear old Gérard. But probably inevitable. And probably the best thing. Were Amedea and he getting so wild at parties because they sensed that the institution was stronger than anything they could feel, no trumpet they could blow would bring down the walls of Jericho? Anyway, Anthony was fairly sanguine these days. But the rataplan was being beaten stirringly.

It had not worked, Amedea insisted. She had tried. Honestly she had tried. She had taught the boy to fish for *gho*. Naturally Francesca knew what *gho* were – but did Anthony and Gérard? Just filthy little fish that swam in the canals, old women fed them to their cats. Well, as a child she had been an enthusiastic catcher of *gho* and now . . . Guy was forever teaching Corrado things, but she didn't seem to know anything to teach, and then she had remembered fishing for *gho*. But it had not worked, God fucking damn it, under no circumstances were they to entertain doubts as to this please, she had been cold. Back in the house at the Miracoli with the Angelica Kauffmann portrait of the Lezze lady who had heard Goethe's table-talk. At the water-gate of that house, with Corrado with a line and hook, fishing for *gho* – but cold. With Gérard and Francesca sitting in the garden and talking and talking because, Amedea in

Anthony's kitchen sneered lightly to their faces, these days they told each other everything, those two, like good boys and girls. Ah yes, a funny thing – in that Kauffmann portrait, had they noticed the plumed hat Marcella Lezze had laid beside her on the balustrade? As a girl, for years Amedea had not realised that it was a hat. That silvery bundle of swirls and fluffs – a Pekingese? she had wondered. A duck-billed platypus wearing a feather boa? Anyhow they had hooked a couple of *gho* for Strassa, Corrado had been cheerful. Happy to be playing with his mother again, she would not deny that, and he adored that cat of his, liked catching her fish. But she had been cold. She swigged her wine. Cold, did they understand? Back in the house with the Marieschi etchings, with the photograph of Captain and Mrs Ashmanhaugh on the steps of Rangoon church, cold. Years ago in pique she had chucked all the family photographs in a drawer – but Guy had resurrected every aunt. By the way, did Francesca know what had become of her favourite photograph – the one of Claudia and her splashing naked in the fountain at Ca' Zante one night? If Corrado were to have family icons around him, that at least would show him what a grand time they had all had. And another thing, were they aware that *gho* made excellent *risotto*? Curious, was it not? Such filthy little fish. Her tears – weren't they stupid? had anyone a handkerchief? Ah, Gérard was very kind. (Anthony had fumbled politely slowly for his, which, Gérard noticed, was spotless.) Her tears were tears of coldness, they should make no question of that. Coldness, bad nerves. Yes, *risotto di gho* was truly quite good.

Anthony dumped dirty plates into the sink. He was reading *The Wings of the Dove*, he told them over the clatter. He wanted to get to the Venice bit. He always felt better when he got to the Venice bit in books. There was a Venice bit in this book, wasn't there? "And worth a library of London and Paris episodes!" Gérard promised him. "Perseverance!" Francesca cried. It was pleasant to be reassured,

Anthony confessed. With any luck it would be like reading *On the Eve* – such a relief when they got to Venice. People said it was tragic, but he always cheered up.

Then there was another depressing thing, Amedea declared. (Who had not been listening. How could she hear? She had taken a poker, she was riddling the grate of her mind, bashing the iron grate to knock the cinders and ash through. Bash. Anything else she felt? Bash. Anything left to think, to say? Bash. Bash.) The tea company had asked Viola Ashmanhaugh to move out of her house, did they know that? And it appeared she refused to leave the Nilgiri Hills and come to Venice, but she was making a mess of finding a new house. Guy had reported that his mother had no friends left, that people stole from her – the neighbourhood was altering. She forgot names, everything. She never finished her sentences – some of them he couldn't comprehend at all – they were just phrases strung together with dot dot dots. And the ridiculous thing was that Guy had not told her that her daughter-in-law had taken a lover. He had intended to tell her. But her distress would have been so confused and impotent, he had said, his courage had ebbed away.

Gérard murmured that he ought to leave soon. Would Amedea come with him?

Yes, yes, in a few minutes, not yet. When the rain blew over. Did he want her to be soaked? (Not, she growled silently, that it wouldn't be refreshing to get away. Away from worthy Francesca particularly, who now for a year or two would be sumptuous, and then, for ever, a fright. Whom Guy had told about his angel – that still needled.) She would light a cigarette. She would refill her glass. If the evening were fine, she might go out in the *sandolo*. Though for herself – they would hardly believe this – the lagoon was not as enchanting as it had been. They were surprised to hear this from her, eh? But the islands lay in fouler water each year. They were not going to deny it, surely? Fewer and fewer white egret waded. That way they had of dipping their heads was lovely. But with all the filth that got pumped into the lagoon, leached and spilled into it, that summer again it would be awash with dead fish and clogged with algae, there'd be a plague of mosquitoes like every year. One could scarcely even find the deserted islands romantic any longer, in her view. All those ruined fortifications, ruined boatsheds, roofless cottages, decayed wharves, nettle-beds. And the scum – creeks of thick green scum rumpled like brocade, with oily glints. And plastic bags that snagged on the trees at high tide, hung there when it went down.

She wanted to go soon, Amedea said to Gérard. Bewildered, he got to his feet. He was ready, he said. No, it was unbearable how he failed to understand her, she groaned. To sea, she had meant. To Greece. And she picked up an ashtray, tipped the ash out on the table. Oh look what she had done, she was sorry, but she knew this, it was Claudia's sprite wasn't it?

A bronze Art Deco lily with a sprite sprawled along the rim. Anthony said he was glad he had at least got the library table and Claudia's sprite from Ca' Zante. Of course there had been other things he would have liked. Books with fine armorial bindings, come from some cardinal's library once maybe. And Revett's *Antiquities of Ionia*, Wood's *Palmyra* – oh yes, handsome books to take down, to leaf through . . . but expensive, it had turned out.

Dish-cloth in hand, Anthony remembered Ralph. Had Amedea? he wondered. Perhaps she had in her slanting way, because she had started mourning Nancy Goncharov, her other dead friend. Sad, Nancy's court, her rag tag and bobtail court, dispersed now. And she had taken Corrado to the Museo Navale – one of her attempts to be a good mother. He liked the models of sailing ships, liked the torpedo – and they had found Nancy's gondola. Astonishing! Had any of them known it was there? The latest acquisition, proudly displayed. That boat they had all often been in. Did they understand? They were all ghosts. Or she at least had no doubt about being one. In a museum. Dead. A bit young, didn't they think?

Zenobia had been built between the wars. She had teak decks, a teak cockpit, and a bowsprit which, like her mast, was pine.

One or two of the other moored yachts had people on board, not more. The sailing-club sheds and slipway were deserted. The marina water had dust floating on its dirtiness. From those smears of oil, those bobbing odds and ends, reflected sunlight rose and shimmered on hulls.

Gérard and Amedea came staggering on board burdened with their last fresh food – bread, meat, bags of vegetables, a bag of peaches. The cabin was stifling, the bunks were piled with clobber not yet stowed. They rammed packages into the fridge till the door would not close.

Gérard had a black eye, which throbbed. This was because in a bar late the night before someone had tried to pick Amedea up, had behaved without courtesy, without respect, and Gérard had started a fight he had quickly lost. For Amedea had two bad reputations by then. For surrendering her child without a quarrel and without betraying grief she was a disgrace to her sex, hardly a woman at all. And for treating her lover high-handedly she was probably an easy lay.

Amedea started the auxiliary engine, came on deck, helped cast off warps, take in fenders. Gérard talked about the Yugoslav islands he wanted to go to, Greek islands, Turkish islands. And what about putting into Split as they sailed south, he had never seen Diocletian's palace, had she?

Yes, as a girl, Amedea said. A sortie to Split had been

one of her father's and her escapes from her mother. But to hell with the emperor Diocletian, she protested, putting the cutter's engine into gear, they were just leaving one ruin, why head straight for another one? And to hell, she thought but did not say, with islands. To hell even with her beloved Venetian islands hitched together with bridges, wasn't it good not to have her feet on them any more, to see the wharf recede twenty yards, fifty? And as for Ionian island shores and Aegean island shores – they were acceptable if they bore no houses or roads, if you anchored in a bay for a day and a night and then sailed on. They were splendid if you sailed by at nightfall in the offing and they disappeared and you sailed on. What she asked aloud was: Had Gérard noticed that the light in the marina was land-light, hazy and golden? But she longed for sea-light harsh with salt, brilliant with cleanliness, in which they would sail through the weeks to come.

Zenobia left the decaying fort of Sant'Andrea to port, then the church of San Nicolò to starboard. Children were playing under the trees by the tideway.

All over the lagoon ordinary things were going on. The caretaker of the abandoned hospital on the island of Sacca Sessola was scything beneath his pear trees and acacia trees. On the island of Burano, long light *gondolini*, one painted white, another blue, others green and orange and red and brown, hauled up on the grass, turned upside down, were being polished for the regatta that afternoon – polished by, among others, the boatbuilder Marco Zanon. In the garden at the Miracoli, Corrado Ashmanhaugh and Signora Donatella were inspecting the geckoes. Throughout the city, herds of people in shorts mooched hither and thither, taking photographs of things, chewing things, licking things. In the ruined Arsenale, Mauro Zanier was standing with a clipboard and a pen, making notes about a roof. On the mainland shore, an oil refinery was volcanoing smoke. On the island of Poveglia, the dogs drowsed.

Guy Ashmanhaugh was not in the Arsenale; he had been

dragooned by Francesca Ziani, whose love and pity were such that he feared she might, when she were older, become a bit of a bully. The *s'ciopon* had left Venice. They had rowed north a long way, past the *valli da pesca* where fish were reared behind mud banks, then out over Palude della Rosa. Marsh lay empty, purple and green and grey. The shallows where they rowed lay empty too, mainly grey, freaked with purple and green weed here and there.

Then the sun came from behind a bar of cloud, and Francesca wanted to cry out because it was so beautiful. Diaphanous swags of a ragged drop-curtain swayed: flamy stippling, traces of white lead. Now the reach they were crossing was washed with blue from the opening sky, slashed with yellow, slashed with pink. Off the shimmer, egret rose. Ahead, Francesca could see Torcello. There stood the rim of trees, the church looking like a barn, the tower, nothing else visible at that range . . . but was Guy at all comforted by the loveliness? Sometimes he said the most depressing things. About all the places which were not places any more, for example, islands where the churches and houses had been pulled down. Like San Giacomo in Palude. Had she seen pictures of that island with a church and quays and vessels and men? he had asked her once. And she had suddenly been sure the dead still rowed there. No doubt the dead rowed away from the island of bones, from Ossario di San Ariano, Francesca had thought – and a cold, wet goose had waddled over her grave. And from San Michele, where the dead were only apparently boxed and slabbed and outlived. No doubt, no doubt. They rowed home to palaces and cottages which were just marsh now, marsh where reeds whispered and salt hay whispered and the tides changed and changed. And they rowed, centuries of the dead, to look for islands that had vanished, gone down, were under the *s'ciopon* now . . .

So it was anxiously that Francesca heard Guy begin to speak.

"Have you ever seen islands being born? It takes a lifetime, but it's worth glimpsing." He told her where – some Indian Ocean atoll, she forgot the name instantly. "The Island Chief and I were crossing the atoll, sailing his old lateen boat among the islands all day. We trailed a fishing line over the stern. Tiny white sand islands, Francesca, with trees, each island in its reef. Some islands with villages, most uninhabited. And there were islands being born. The sea is the colour of lapis lazuli, and when you notice a patch turning turquoise you know an island is coming up. Sail by years later, the turquoise will be opal. It's beautiful, opalescent shallows in the sun. A few years more, and you've got a white shoal. The first comers are the dead, of course." Guy laughed. "Dead turtle, dead ray, dead eel, dead everyone. They're washed up. But then on the white mound you see the first cross-hatchings, sprigs of seedlings. Well, sailing back to my Island Chief's island that day we saw a greenness and a whiteness deep in the blue sea. The Island Chief had his foot on the gunwhale, he gazed overboard, he started to laugh. Good, he said. New island. And near enough to mine, I think. He had four uninhabited islands that lay within sight of his island, he'd send his people over to plant vegetables or to cut down trees to build a boat, so another coming up was cheerful news. He slapped his hand on his knee. This will be my island when it is born, he declared. Francesca, I've never envied any man as I envied that Island Chief then. He clapped my shoulder, went back to his helm. I envied him because out there in the Indian Ocean the sea is very clean. And . . . And I've never seen anything so fresh and naked and clean as those islands when they're born. No history. Then the Island Chief grinned and said, That island will be mine, if I am still alive when it comes up – but I do not think that I shall be alive."

On board *Zenobia*, Amedea was bending on her foresails, hoisting them. Then the mainsail. They fluttered in the wind of the yacht's passage. Looking aft, she saw the tender was not towing right. It slewed from port to starboard and back again. It rushed at the yacht's counter, fell back, veered, rushed at the other side – like Charlie Chaplin, she thought, trying to catch a tram. And now Gérard had noticed, he was adjusting the painter so the tender towed calmly.

In the mouth of the lagoon, swallows were skimming over the water. Offshore, the sails of a regatta flecked the horizon. Away, away! psalmed in Amedea's head as standing on her foredeck she heard Gérard cut the auxiliary, felt quiet come about her. The light wind filled the sails. *Zenobia* headed out between the lighthouses. Away! She could feel the sea's faint lift and fall.

That night, the red and green lights shone stalwartly in the cutter's shrouds. The white masthead light looked ghostly. So did the white sails. Moonlight and starlight were pale on the sea, on the splash of a fish that jumped.

At the helm, Amedea leaned to the binnacle. The compass looked back with a white face.

Sailing south down the Adriatic they had fitful airs. Amedea Lezze longed for burly winds, but they were slight. Often for hours *Zenobia* was becalmed. Once they drifted close to the carcass of a big fish, a tunny maybe, it was hard to tell from the festering mess. It seemed all the vermin of the sea were moseying in it. With the auxiliary, *Zenobia* moved a few hundred yards to where the air was wholesome to breathe, the sea attractive to dive into.

When she was becalmed, rat thoughts scampered round Amedea's cage head. At least they were inching away from Venice – which was a stagnant little place, and had been for a couple of centuries – which was rank cliché, like herself – which deserved its politicians, deserved its tourists – and where people permitted themselves the vulgarity of forming opinions about her. But they were only inching away. And they would have to go back. And that, when you had been staring at the same waste of blue sea half the day, was intolerable. Then a breeze would come. They would trim the sails. The breeze would shift. Then it would die. The new waste of sea would be a mile or two or three from the old waste; but it would look the same. And the sun! It was like being belaboured over the head with a hot frying-pan. Even wearing a hat. Like being belaboured hour-long, when there was no wind.

The setting sun would sit on the horizon like a blood-orange on a shelf. But when it had slowly rolled off backward, had slowly fallen from sight, things got better. Sometimes at nightfall a wind came, *Zenobia* drifted on her way. It was peaceful to eat supper in the cockpit and drink a bottle of wine. Usually they drank more than one bottle of wine. One night phosphorescence spangled around the yacht, licked the tender, clung to the painter where it slacked and sagged. No landfall till they were through the Straits of Otranto, Gérard was made to agree. But after that, if he really wanted to . . . they could put into Murtos, or into Laka maybe. Or they might sail further down the Ionian, make a landfall on the shores of Lefkas or Cephalonia. Amedea did not want ever to set foot on land again. But she would discuss landfalls. It was better than discussing things farther ahead. For of course in Tuscany they had talked endlessly of Guy, of Corrado; and of course they might as well not have done. All would be well, Amedea would say exhaustedly when *Zenobia* was becalmed – or, if not well, bearable. But if Gérard leant forward intently, if he demanded to know how? in what way? she was too irritated by the lifeless sails slatting from side to side, too dazed by the sun glittering on the sea till she knew she had a chip of glass in her eyeball, a chip that burned, too spent to explain that when she dreaded going back to Venice she was chiefly dreading going back to be Guy's wife. His estranged wife. His wife who was much like any other friend, except that her mere existence happened to torture him. Where Corrado was concerned, they would unite . . . Ah God, it was all so obvious! So damned civilised! Guy might spend more time in the East. She might take a flat in Rome. But it would be sensible to spend half the year, say, at the house at the Miracoli, be what she could in the way of a mother . . . More sensible than scudding round art galleries.

No one ever pieced a heaven together like that. Not even when you found yourself at a dead end, and a daft idea of your father's (its charm was lost on her when the yacht was becalmed) seemed a possible way out. And the restaurant tables for one were depressing after a while.

Then one afternoon it blew hard from the north-west. White horses careered over the blue sea, jumping, falling, galloping on. *Zenobia* ran before the wind with her blue spinnaker up, white hull rolling through white spray. And the next day coming through the Straits of Otranto they were in luck again, they had a fine sailing wind on the beam, for a slow old vessel she made good speed for a few hours.

Amedea was at the tiller. She sailed hard, as if she were racing unseen antagonists, she imagined their sails scattered about the sea. She glanced up at the luff of the mainsail, at the burgee blowing against the sky, glanced at the bowsprit plunging at the waves, jumbled seas foaming along the lee rail. She revelled in the blown sunlight and blown spume. And there was Gérard winching in the jib sheet. His hay hair, after days of salt and sun, was turning to straw. He is steadfast, he understands! Amedea rejoiced. I shanghaied him to Tuscany. Now I've shanghaied him again. We are lovers! she rejoiced (the yacht was bowling over the waves, the sun was hot, her heart was high.) My marriage is too depressing to talk about, but Gérard is steadfast, he understands, look at him winching away! *Zenobia* shouldered a comber; spindrift came flying over the weather rail and soaked Amedea's hair, her shirt, her shorts. She flinched, she laughed, she licked the salt off her mouth.

The wind dropped, dropped, died away.

Look at me! Amedea despaired. Blown by the winds, becalmed by the calms.

"Land!" she demanded. "All right, don't look at me with such amazement, I can change my mind can't I?"

Gérard was rigging the awning. If they could not sail, shade in the cockpit would be good. "Where do you want to go?"

"*Anywhere!*" she cried, and tried to laugh. "Anywhere deserted. We'll use up some fuel, it doesn't matter. I'm going to have a look at the chart."

A reef ran offshore, they saw it on the chart, and they saw water breaking when they came gliding inshore with a zephyr in the canvas and then under the lee of the island it was nearly dead calm and they heard the cicadas and they saw the bay was rock that side, bad holding for the anchor. Toward the other shore the sea was pale over sand and a beach gleamed. The bay was sheltered from the north. It was open to the south; but weeks might pass and a scirocco never blow. A hundred yards from the beach, Gérard headed the cutter up into what faint wind there was, losing way, losing way. When *Zenobia* lay still, Amedea lowered the anchor. Why did the anchor dropping down the bow and then into the water make her think of an angel falling? she fretted. Damned jittery, she was getting. But so it was. The spread curving flukes were iron wings outspread. The angel was hanged sadistically by her heels, lowered away.

"If the weather changes," Gérard remarked, "we can lay out the kedge anchor too."

"If the weather changes, we'll put out to sea. Safer, my darling. And a lot more fun."

Then it was affectionate to stand either side of the boom, taking battens out of the mainsail, furling the sail along the spar. They passed sail-ties to one another across the furls, made fast, handed the next. It was good to feel the setting sun glance off the water on to your salty skin, good that there were swifts towering, good then to drink a glass of whiskey with cold water in it and watch the midges dance.

The hillside was rock and scrub and dust, buzzard wheeled overhead, cormorant on boulders below the bluff stretched their wings. If you climbed you could reach terraces where olives had been planted and had grown well, but had not been pruned for ten years or more, so the gnarled trees would crop poorly. The terraces had not been maintained. Years of rain were making them lose stones from their parapets, lose soil, lose definition. Now at midsummer the olives were small, green, hard. The only sound was the cicada clamour, except once, carried on the flittering breeze, Gérard and Amedea thought they heard goat bells, but then the breath veered.

The terraces were barricaded with gorse, with juniper. Butterflies rose as the lovers pushed through: White Admirals, Swallow-tails. From the abandoned olive grove you could look down through the boughs and see the bay and some lesser coves and the white cutter alone in the anchorage with the big Italian flag at her stern. You could not tell it was the Italian flag at that distance, and the Greek courtesy flag at the crosstree was too small to be seen. But from the hill you could distinguish clearly where the bay was light blue over sand and the holding was as good as you were going to get, where it lay purplish over weed that would foul the best-designed anchor.

"After being at sea," Amedea asked, "doesn't the land seem very hard, very rough?" She laughed. "And so dry! And it never moves – not at all lively. I shall pray for an earthquake. Nothing murderous. But the earth could shrug a little, couldn't it, gaily?" And she remembered the Friuli earthquake, the crumpled villages, the dead; and miles away in Venice, her chandelier swinging wildly. So she launched herself slithering down a bank, picked herself up, brushed her clothes, her hands. "Look, dust. I'd forgotten what it feels like." What else could she think of that would sound gay? "My dreams have been getting dull. As entertainment, they're a disgrace. If we sleep on shore, do you think they might be startled into a bit more subtlety?" But Gérard was not paying attention, damn him. He had found a tortoise, wanted to show it to her. And yes, she agreed, it was an admirable tortoise, charming. But, dear God, could he not at least have – oh, she didn't know! but something – could he not have suggested – what?

That night the land was hospitable, after sunset the scrub entertained them with fireflies. When Gérard and Amedea wandered among the jigging sparks, they trod on herbs and crushed them and made the air pungent. They brought sleeping-bags ashore. But sprawled in moonlight on the beach, looking at *Zenobia* out in the bay, Amedea drank so much wine that next day she didn't know if she had dreamed.

No wind rose. Gérard went to climb crags. Amedea lay naked on the sand, she lay naked in the shallows. Becalmed again! Why had she not forseen? Ashore, you'd be becalmed even if the wind blew. Nothing could save you.

She put on her straw hat; she sauntered in the shallows; she kicked the ripples in a small, regular, futile way, like walking a suburban street kicking leaves. Time ground creaking through her mind as slowly as a hawser ground in through a fairlead. Amedea stopped stock-still to stare at the accoutrements of the idle woman discarded among sea shells: half read novel, dark glasses, bathing dress. So this was it, was it? The treachery you had done, you tried to undo. She would go back to Guy, who would not want her, who would accept her, who was immobilised by sadness (had he *no* power of resurgence? but perhaps it would take years). After rain, she would go down to the water-gate of the house at the Miracoli, she would bail out the *s'ciopon*, sitting on the gunwhale in the cobwebby water-dazzle of new sun on façades, on canal, on bridges, sitting and bailing and shading her eyes, calling back when neighbours and boatmen called. (It would be preferable to long colloquies with Guy or Donatella. Bailing alone, for the soul of dishonour, would be preferable.) Yes, this was it. This was how it went. The passion you had begun in joy, you abandoned in dismay. Gérard had scrambled down from his screes, he stood beside her now in the shallows, splashing off the dust. But Amedea had not the courage to tell him. Becalmed, she stood up to her calves in the Ionian, she chewed her mouth. He talked about a spring he had found.

That night the fireflies went elsewhere, or they were finished for the year. The sky clouded over, a southerly wind blew up, the sleepers on the sand were woken by waves. *Zenobia* was tossing in dawn murk. Rafts of seaweed were driving ashore, banking up. All the insects on the bay had blown ashore, Amedea had never seen such grey hordes crawling and winging. Up the hill, the olive grove was in tumult; it kept changing colour, because the gusts pitchforked the foliage so the green leaves showed their grey undersides. The cormorants' rocks had vanished under breakers, spray was scending into the scrub.

Rowing out in the tender, Gérard and Amedea were drenched. The cutter's anchor was holding, the donkey-engine started, they got out to sea. Amedea was cheerful: they ought to get some wild sailing toward Kithera.

But that day the wind faded again. It left a vicious slop.

Zenobia could once more be degraded to a motorboat, they could chug ignobly along. Or they could lie rolling in the ugly broken seas.

Zenobia idled south down the coast of Peleponnisos: a few hours of passage, a few hours becalmed. Often at night they forgot whose watch it was. It was good to sit in the cockpit together while the yacht ghosted on through the darkness, and it was finest of all to make love on deck at night. Lying in her lover's arms, looking up past the sails, picking out Arcturus or Vega or Cassiopeia, who would not, Amedea Lezze demanded petulantly of the constellations, long for things to last? long helplessly, she supposed, for immortality – was that the heart of it? But then she heard singing in her head: *These precious days I'll spend with you.* And to be the prey of sentimental old songs was unbearable; it was a more vile mockery than to be the prey of sentimental old longings for transcendence. Brusquely she disentangled herself from Gérard's arms, she stood up. Nonsense that had been felt in vain before – why could she feel nothing else? The adulterous longings and the maternal longings and guilts – all cliché! I am a squab, she decided. A grey, squashy, naked, quilled squab. And to me, to my ugliness in the shitty nest, comes the fond, pretty dove of the past, and regurgitates pap from her beak to my beak.

She was more cheerful on deck, Amedea discovered without bothering to feel ashamed, when Gérard was below, asleep for preference. One evening a storm was flickering in the north, too far off for thunder to be heard. Even an hour later, when a second storm began to flash in the south, she didn't wake him to admire the show. It was sheet lightning not forked lightning, the second storm, a shutter in the sky that opened and blazed a moment and closed. The cutter hung motionless, lightning leaping astern, lightning flaring ahead. Amedea lay on the dewy deck. A block knocked in the quietness; the sails shivered, were still. When the northerly storm stopped doing its harum scarum dashes, when the southerly shutter in the sky was latched, it was time to wake Gérard. But she didn't wake him.

When the dawn airs were wafting through the grey, over the grey, when the burgee began to twiddle, Amedea stood up. She took off her clothes, stepped to the gunwhale, dived. She came up, she tossed her head, she swam hard, a fast crawl. But then she looked back over her shoulder. A breath had filled the sails. *Zenobia* was moving away.

Swimming back furiously, she saw Gérard come into the cockpit, bring the cutter round. She laughed, swallowed a mouthful of Ionian, choked, swam on more calmly. She got her hands to the rope ladder, her feet. Being helped dripping over the gunwhale, "What woke you up?" she asked.

"I wasn't asleep. I . . . I heard you dive."

He handed her a towel. Thin, panting, she rubbed herself. "You keep a bloody good eye on me, don't you?" And then, leaning to haul the rope ladder back on board, she said, "You know, this won't last. We'll come to grief, you and I."

Quiet! Gérard's mind prayed. Still! Quiet! What's the good of a miracle if you're not true to it? Let her go. Let her go.

They did not, as Gérard Charry wished to, put into Navarino Bay where you could see ships of the Turkish fleet sunk at the Battle of Navarino lying on the bed of the sea. And they were off Cape Matapan – Amedea remembered Donatella's boy husband drowned forty years before – when the weather broke.

Clouds piled up, thick, grey. Still no wind rose. The sea slopped. Then it rained. The rain cascaded down the air, it sluiced down the mast, it sluiced down the sails, poured off the boom, over the cabin, down the scuppers. Gérard and Amedea stayed on deck, being beaten by the deluge. They made love.

In the Aegean it blew hard, Amedea was excited. They laid a course north-east to pass through the Cyclades. Gérard wanted to reach Mitilini off the Turkish coast, go ashore, look at the acropolis.

Amedea just wanted to sail. The scirocco raged from the south-east, a Cretan wind, an Egyptian wind. It must have started dry and hot. It battened on *Zenobia* in sodden squalls on the starboard beam. Amedea insisted they carry more sail than was wise; the cutter made heavy weather of it, shipped breaking seas over the foredeck.

First *Zenobia*'s mistress longed to get among the islands. When they raised Milos over the horizon on a foul evening, she yelled "There it is! Land ahoy!" like a child, Gérard thought. She charged down the companion-way, came up with two glasses of Irish, gave him one. She raised her glass. Her grey eyes were bright. Her tangled bob whipped about her face. "Don't you think this passage is glorious?" she cried.

Then each island was a milestone she had to thrash past, a storm-obscured outcrop in the Greek sea she had to leave astern. When this passion of hers had winched Gérard's nerves almost to snapping, it was all the Cyclades she wanted to cast behind her, she needed open sea.

During Gérard's watch, Amedea was often on deck, trying to glory in the turbulent seaway and labouring cutter as fervently as she gloried when he was on his bunk. She hardly troubled any longer to conceal that she preferred him to be below decks, and this scared him. He would lie in the gloom on his swaying, juddering bunk and imagine her at the helm, how she was rejoicing in the storm unconfinedly, rejoicing in her solitude.

Reefing was simpler done in daylight. Amedea insisted only one reef was necessary. This meant they had a rough ride that night, and had to take in a second reef next day.

With the mainsail reefed right down, *Zenobia* sailed more easily, but then the wind rose again. They cleared the Cyclades, Amedea was exuberant, Tinos fell astern. They had no dry clothes left, but wind and spindrift were warm. They had given up cooking. They ate biscuits. Gérard had given up shaving.

He felt utterly weary. Huddled on the leeward bunk, trying to rest, trying not to sleep long or deeply, he would drowse for an hour, clamber up to the cockpit to check that Amedea was all right, shame-facedly offer to sail the rest of her watch. When she said she was fine, he would stumble down the companion-way again. Back on his damp bunk, he would pray for Amedea to be less hysterical about sailing. He would pray that the wind might drop so *Zenobia* would stop bashing, lurching, shuddering, so there might be peace. His cuts and bruises ached.

The following nightfall, Gérard was steering. "Something will break if we go on like this," he said. Amedea was happy (Venice was far astern, the wind was strong, she was in love today, and as for tomorrow!) she did not mock his good sense, she bounded forward along the sidedeck. She lowered the staysail. It struggled like a maddened creature in her arms. Gérard was afraid. The bucking foredeck was trying to throw her off, the sail would carry her away. He shouted, "Don't bother with the sail-bag!" Amedea grinned merrily. A big sea hit the bow, she vanished in spume, then Gérard saw she was still there, hanging onto a stanchion. Laughing, she rammed the staysail under the foredeck shock-cords along the rail. She decided to leave the storm-jib up, scrambled back to the cockpit.

That night when it was Amedea's watch she insisted Gérard try to sleep. He told her, "Stay in the cockpit. If you have to go forward, use a life-line." He handed her the glass of whiskey she asked for; then he lay down.

Zenobia pitched and rolled, she danced, Amedea felt she was dancing too. The wind sang in the shrouds. Amedea sang, though she couldn't hear her songs – for was not freedom welling up from her heart, up her throat, hosannahing in her triumphant head? White horses galloped alongside, she liked it when they reared and tossed their manes.

Amedea decided not to wake Gérard for his watch. He lay as if in a coma, no crashing of the hull reached him, she let the chronometer on the cabin bulkhead tick past his hour. She did not want to miss a moment of sailing on a night so wild. The gale must blow itself out tomorrow or the next day. Too soon. Then she saw she had left the jib up too long, it was tattering at the leech.

Zenobia would sail for a few minutes with her helm lashed, Amedea ought to have time, she climbed out of the cockpit. The staysail was jerking free of its shock-cords, she would have to stow it again and stow it properly this time. A comber came on board, knocked her slithering. She picked herself up, went on.

Jib halyard. Outhaul running back from the bowsprit. Hard to see in the night and the spray. Maybe she should have woken Gérard to help. How badly was that storm-jib torn? The masthead light staggered. No moon, no stars. Her fingers were clumsy at the cleats. The sail came down, half of it fell overboard, the other half cannonaded to leeward.

The bowsprit went into a black crest. Amedea clung to the pulpit with one hand, the downhaul with the other, lost her footing when the wave rolled over her, lay flat on her face gasping while it roared and shattered away.

She heaved herself up, got her hands to the jib-sheet, then to the jib. *Zenobia*'s bow climbed in the darkness, teetered sickeningly, came thundering down.

The jib in Amedea's arms filled with wind. She trod on the staysail, slipped, the rail hit her behind her knees. She grabbed for the bowsprit, missed.

Gérard did not know what woke him, but he knew he was afraid. Then he heard canvas banging, he felt *Zenobia* tossing out of control. Stumbling up the companion-way, a hundredweight of water hit him on the head, crashed over the chart table.

He thought Amedea must be somewhere, he could not lose her like this, he cried her name. He scrambled about the boat like a mad animal – but *Zenobia* was so small! – jerking his head to stare. She couldn't be lost, he didn't understand, he did understand. The staysail was flogging on the foredeck. The jib was dragging alongside, but Amedea was not clinging to it.

Gérard could not scramble about the sea, that was the hideous thing. There the sea heaved and broke blackly. But how could he search it for her, hunt up and down those hills of water till she were found? At least, the sea must be heaving and breaking blackly. He could hear its roar. But he could only see a few feet around the yacht's gunwhales.

Zenobia was not clambering about the sea, she was being pitched this way and that. Gérard crouched on the cabin, ducking when the boom slammed across, choking when a wave soused him. The cutter must be made to clamber again. He shut the hatch over the companion-way. He would have to get to the pump soon. He freed the helm. Why wouldn't the damned boat sail, so he could look for

Amedea and find her and hold her in his arms? He stared around. He was weeping with frustration, not yet with grief. Astern, the tender had swamped. That was a sea-anchor all right. And how could he salvage her? He could cut the painter if he could find his knife. He scrabbled at the cleat, it took a minute, two minutes, he cast the little hulk adrift.

But he did not want to sail anywhere. It was here that Amedea had gone overboard. Fallen overboard. Or jumped, that crossed his mind. She had been pretty ecstatic all the day, all the storm, all the passage through the Cyclades – and had wanted him below decks – and – no, no! he mustn't think that.

She might only have gone over the side five minutes ago. Why did the engine have to be underwater, a wreck? How long could a swimmer last in those tumbling seas? At least it was warm. Amedea might be floundering very close. He screamed her name till his voice cracked. The wind shrieked. There was a life-belt in a locker, Gérard snatched it out. There was a flare pistol. He fired it. Fireworks, he thought. The flare described its paradisal flight, it didn't have the deathliness of material things till it fell. He pulled the trigger again. Whiteness soared up and shuddered and hung in the sky and blew away. Fireworks Amedea my sweet love, do you remember the Festa del Redentore and the fleet of Venetian craft that night and you and I in the *sandolo* and fireworks falling on the lagoon?

Zenobia sailed in circles. At least, Gérard tried to sail in circles, roughly. Staring at the sea. Calling, and staring at the sea. The worst was when he saw what he thought might be Amedea and tried to tack toward her, he yelled, he was mad with love and hope, but the cutter would not tack without a jib and by the time she tacked it was too late. Because the shadow on the black or the trick of the mind or the dead woman or the swirl of spume had gone.

It would be easier when dawn came. He could search the sea all day. If the gale slacked it would be easier. What should he do when the next night fell? The circles in which

Gérard tried to sail and failed were drifting down-wind. *Zenobia* would not beat up against the storm under only a reefed mainsail. He would have to get a foresail up, if they were not all ripped. Amedea must be being flung before the scirocco too. Any undamaged foresail he hoisted would rip soon. Amedea must be being hurled up on each wave and hurled forward and rolled deep.

Guy Ashmanhaugh learned of his wife's death in a telegram from Piraeus. Then a long letter came.

Corrado cried when his father told him his mother had been drowned, but then he cheered up. Thereafter all Guy knew was that he could not know what shadows had started to gather in the child's mind, and would always be gathering.

Gérard Charry sailed back to Venice in *Zenobia*. It was September. He asked if he might come to the house at the Miracoli. Guy and Francesca had expected him to be nervous; but they were shocked by the haggard, fleshless creature who stood in the *salone* being looked at by the picture of Marcella Lezze.

Gérard took the key to the cutter's cabin from his pocket, held it out. He had had the sails repaired, he said; and the engine worked again; and he would like to pay for a new tender. Guy told him not to be an idiot. Anyhow, he tried to ask laughingly, he hadn't got rich all of a sudden, had he? They were both blushing now, each standing islanded on a rug. Gérard muttered that of course he hadn't, but he was selling his *sandolo*.

No one blamed him for anything, Guy insisted. They were all sorry for him. He was sorry for him. He guessed he must have had a foul time with the Greek police. Yes,

Gérard replied, for weeks. But searching the sea all day had been worse, and then deciding he had to give up. Guy shook him by the hand, got him out of the door. He thought Gérard might say things it would be embarrassing to listen to. They said goodbye in the street. Francesca told Gérard he was not to disappear, they were his friends. He said he had applied for a job in Africa. He turned to go, wavered. There was something, he said, blushing again. Something he felt Guy ought to know. Amedea had decided to come back to him, if she had lived she would have come back. Then Gérard walked away, Guy and Francesca went back into the house. They were alone there. Signora Donatella had declared she did not wish to meet Gérard Charry. She had gone shopping with the child he believed he had orphaned.

At the boatyard, Signor Gastone asked Gérard if he were buying a more glamorous vessel, a *puparin* possibly? No, Gérard answered, I'm leaving Venice, I can't have a boat here any more. The man who was buying the *sandolo* laid his cheque-book on the thwart and wrote. Take that iron-work off the transom, he said, so we can fit a bracket for an outboard engine. On the slipway, the vat of tar had been lifted off the brazier. The men were grilling fish for their lunch. They poured out wine. Cats fought over fish guts. Signor Gastone fetched a chisel, wrenched at the transom of the *sandolo*. Gérard put the cheque in his pocket. He watched the chisel. Then he could not bear to watch, so he turned away and called goodbye Signor Gastone and walked out of the boatyard.

An hour before daybreak he was still wandering. He crossed Accademia bridge, came into Campo Santo Stefano. He remembered rowing beneath the church floor. At the far end of the square, three figures were sitting at a table outside Paolin. Two men and a woman, with a candelabra.

Slowly, Gérard walked. More slowly still. Guy Ashmanhaugh and Francesca Ziani belonged together, he thought.

They were not in love; but they had gentleness and trust. And Anthony Holt belonged with them and they with him.

Gérard stood still, unnoticed, hesitating. Then he turned aside, toward San Maurizio. He left the three friends sitting in the dim square under the autumn stars, with their candles flickering.

Five

There was, it turned out, Francesca Ziani thought three years later, an epilogue. For Guy and she were engaged.

The wedding was to be at the Municipio, not in church. And certainly the occasion would be as devoid of glamour as of mysticism: just her parents, Corrado, Anthony Holt . . . And the painters, of course. Two wedding presents had been planned, that she knew of (and doubtless Anthony would turn up with an Ignatius Loyola second edition, or Sarah Bernhardt's writing case, or . . .). Franco Tagliapietra had promised her one of his lagoon skies, to hang beside the one he had given Guy years before. And Etienne Maas was painting her portrait.

Francesca had already been to sit the first time. It had been a cloudy autumn day. She had sat near Etienne's window over the Giudecca Canal, a few feet from where Ralph Chedgrave had been Death leaning on his scythe, and Etienne had made a pot of tea. While he painted, they had talked. Etienne still gave as good parties as ever, but these days they tended to be dinner parties for a dozen not dances for a hundred. And judging by his first day's work, her portrait was going to be downright respectable – which, Francesca mused, was probably appropriate, for Venice, that muddy village twittery with opinion, had been expecting this marriage for some while. Etienne had posed her in a plain white shirt, sitting with her hands in her lap. Not so much as a necklace. What would give brilliance to the painting would be the blue and red and silver stuff of the curtain behind her, the marble façade of the Gesuati seen across the water far away. But she was not brilliant. She was peaceful, she was strong, she was at the heart of things. (Perhaps she had mistaken Etienne's intention. Many sittings would be needed. But her first impression had been unequivocal.) His canvases were selling quite profitably these days, Etienne had told her as he painted, nudes and brides alike, so she had been pleased for him. He was going to be able to have new window frames in the studio, and a proper bathroom with hot water, all manner of luxuries. And she had sat there, beginning to look matronly already at twenty-three, and listened to him, and sipped her tea. And Gérard Charry had never written, nobody knew where he had fetched up. Francesca was still astonished by how completely Amedea and he had vanished. They had simply gone – like rain falling on sea.

Standing in the *salone* of the Lezze house at the Miracoli (an old shell of the hermit crab's, she thought) Francesca brought to mind Gérard who had never written. Then Donatella, who was in hospital; who had wept when Guy and she had told her they were engaged, had wept and held their hands and blessed them; who might live till their wedding next month but, her doctor had warned them, might not. Then Corrado, who looked more like Amedea every year; who could tell Doric from Ionic from Corinthian at a glance; but who might, Francesca had worried more than once lately, have inherited some of his mother's airs and graces, judging by the bruises he sometimes came back from school with. Then that mother herself – no doubt stuck now, poor camel, her long thin limbs struggling, in the eye of the needle. No, nowhere to go beyond the eye, for Amedea. Francesca stood still, frowned, tried to concentrate, tried to bring to life the true Amedea. I want the true shadow, the true vagueness, she thought, not one with a superficial resemblance to it merely. She would focus on the table before her, get that clear. She looked. A pile of Guy's architecture journals; Corrado's homework, and a model of a galley; her own Svevo thesis, nearly finished now . . . It is common ground, the *salone* table, she observed; we meet here, we three. But now with this focus to raise one's head, see Amedea . . . It was impossible! she moaned. She could not do it; she had to admit she could not. (For the seeds of humility that at nineteen she had felt sprouting in her mulch greymatter had grown well; she was a modest person.) Anything might be true! Nothing was truer than anything else. She didn't know. The bullet-proof black Mercedes of Amedea's soul, flanked by outriders, had been waved through the traffic of the flesh, for all Francesca knew, had swept on its way – where? – anywhere – nowhere . . .

Perhaps she was not quite so modest a person as all that, because on occasion she had imagined her humility to be a hat. That was a foolish way she'd had of bolstering her confidence. She could see that hat now, lying on the table with the model galley which Corrado had spent she did not know how many afternoons piecing together, and Strassa who had just leaped up and wanted to have her head rubbed. A new straw hat with a wide brim, her hat of humility, a hat so dark a blue that it was black with blue luminescences. She stretched out one hand (the other was tickling Strassa's black ears) and picked it up, her hat of nothing, hat of the mind. The dyed straw was slightly rough, slightly hard, on the pads of her fingers. She was so pleased with her hat – it must have been the swirl of silk knotted around the crown, or the handsome rose pinned there – that she put it on, she was a girl dressing up to play charades all on her own. She sauntered to the looking-glass, she thought she might see if with a different length of silk . . .

But she would not require such flamboyant humility when she was the second Mrs Ashmanhaugh – or the first, in a way, because her cousin, Francesca now recalled, had never used that name. Indeed, she would consign her hat to a cupboard right now. Amused to be restless – for who had ever been fortunate like her? she marvelled, who happy like her?– she drifted upstairs.

There were so many things to be done! And they would all be happy things. As soon as her thesis was finished, she must look for a job. And Guy and she had agreed they really would make a start at restoring the house – begin with the roof – of course it would take years – and it would be so expensive, they would have to go cautiously – but a start! And the house would be happy once more (Guy promised his headaches were far less frequent these days) and would be shared by Corrado and by their children who would be born.

Here was the wardrobe where a few dresses of Amedea's that had been too glorious to throw away still hung – and one or two older things, the dress by Fortuny, the dress by Poiret to be worn with a turban, and here the faded turban was, Francesca noticed, tossing her abstract, fabulous head-gear on to a shelf carelessly, because Amedea did not matter any more. No doubt she had not been the only spoilt woman to take her lover on a yacht that summer. Probably she had not been the only one to meet with an accident. And how like her to run away to sea with her sweetheart! Hopelessly old-fashioned. Dishearteningly unoriginal. How like the woman to fall overboard in a storm! Melodramatic to the last. Drunk, as likely as not. What else remained to be said? It was good of her, that night, to warn me that I didn't have to inherit Guy and Corrado and the Miracoli if I didn't want to, Francesca thought. But I did want to. And now I rejoice in her self-denial, in her gift to me. (Misunderstandings, which are the incisors of oblivion, and which had been nibbling at these events, these feelings, were beginning to take bigger bites.) Oh yes, and it was kind of Gérard to tell Guy that his wife intended to return to him . . . but, surely, a kind lie. And if she had returned, it would have been a frigid household for Corrado to grow up in. But what on earth is this stench? And this hissing noise?

For Francesca had not stayed in her bedroom, she had wandered on, and now stood in the door of Corrado's room. Guy had given his son a model of an early steam engine. It was made of steel, it was painted red and green, it had a brass funnel, a brass whistle. They were kneeling shoulder to shoulder in a fog of steam and a reek of methylated spirits. Guy glanced around, smiled at her, winked, went back to trying to coax the engine into action. Yes, these days he smiles, his fiancée thought. He is above all, perhaps, relieved (he is doing the right thing by the woman who dedicated herself to his child). I hope they make their machine go. I hope it doesn't explode – can all that steam be right? I hope they don't scald themselves.

Francesca climbed the attic stair. Here was the *altana*. Guy and she had replaced the rotten timbers; the platform and railings were safe now; you could tread, you could lean. They had lugged new terracotta urns up there, they had trained the jasmin and honeysuckle. The autumn dusk was mild, was still. She was at peace. Almost, almost there was no more agitation inside her head or outside, almost there was no more noise now – except the last swifts whirling and skirling. Ah yes and away on the mainland an aeroplane was banking sharply skyward, and from their neighbour's roof music was seeping, the melody oozed in deformed mews up through the tiles – but maybe it had been ugly to start with.

Roofs, roofs. And I have the Miracoli dome for company, Francesca thought. (A banshee shriek below made her jump. Ah, that damned steam engine. Clearly the whistle worked.) And here in this *sestiere* she would set up her peace. (She could see the roof of the hospital where probably she would have her baby.) Here in this house, on this *altana* where for years with Donatella she had pegged up clothes to dry and tasted the wooden taste of the pegs she held in her lips . . . Here, she murmured – the word becoming a talisman. Here. Here.

The Venice that Amedea Lezze and Gérard Charry left had not altered much, Francesca reflected. Politicking and speculation still bedevilled the place, now and then a church was restored, the wreck of the Serene Republic was commercially exploited with slightly ghastlier vulgarity every year, the Venetians kept draining away to the mainland. The shops for tourists had not yet appeared along what had been Gérard's quay – you could still get a bookcase dovetailed there, or a balcony cast – though they would. She believed there were still a few lunatics, if they were lunatics, in the handsome madhouse on the island of San Clemente. At San Nicolò dei Mendicoli the old seaman still kept apes, though she had heard he was ill. The old man from Malamocco still rowed over to the ruins and thickets of Poveglia to feed the abandoned dogs. She wouldn't be surprised, Francesca thought, if Amedea's dead weren't still sitting in a huddle of nineteenth-century wheelchairs in their ruined hospital. Certainly in some hazy sense the Angel of Melancholy still sat on the littoral. On blue days you might still see parachutes appear over the Lido. When a breeze came to the garden of the Hotel des Bains, the Jazz Age palm trees shimmied as they used to do. Naturally there had been small changes here and there. Nancy Goncharov's ill-grown palace was a gallery. But for the most part things had drifted sluggishly on. Everybody still discussed whether or not they were to have movable barriers at the lagoon mouths to keep out flood tides; whether these would further diminish trade to the port, which was in decline as it had been for years.

Those who gloried in the transitory had disappeared; those who fumbled to patch up edifices and institutions were still here; everything was as it should be. Only Corrado hadn't yet done his homework – and now he was happy playing with his engine – and oh dear, soon she'd have to make him sit down – and he would sigh, and kick the table leg. "Francesca, I can't do this bit," he would say. And she would tell him, "Do what you can. We'll do the difficult bits together at the end." Poor Corrado. But never mind. What had she been wondering about? Francesca began picking dead leaves off the *altana* geraniums. (In County Clare, Claudia Glaven was walking her Labradors. In Paris, a retired professor was writing a letter to his son in what had been a French colonial town in West Africa.) And who had Francesca bumped into the other day but Cecilia Zancana? Expensively dressed, pushing a pram, chinking her bracelets, chucking her black curls. She had introduced her to her husband: well-cut suit, well-cut moustaches, a watch only young directors of several companies wear – perfect. Cecilia had given her a straight look she had liked and had asked if she had had word of Gérard Charry. Gérard who, Francesca recalled – it made her smile as she spruced up her flowers – could always tell you how the Servi nuns were getting on with their vegetable garden. And it might have been his boat she had glimpsed last week, or it might have been any blue and grey *sandolo* vanishing down a canal. Anyway there was undoubtedly a lot of good in Cecilia. If she had not had the nerve to break her engagement, at least she conducted her marriage cheerfully. And yes, certainly she would visit them in Como one day, Francesca had promised. How wonderful! Really, did their new flat have a view over the lake?

The wild had been put to flight; the tame were inheriting the earth. And she would never again mind, Francesca determined, that Amedea had considered that fetching from school and instilling table manners and ironing shirts were about her level. Nor would she be made anxious by Guy's record of despairing of his first marriage; of paying attention to the bickering on the Tower of Babel, the difficulties, of giving up. Her expectations were modest. Only – it was strange . . . When she tried to imagine the forgotten, the utterly dispelled, those gone out of our ken . . . When she tried to imagine those of whom the last misleading notion was wisping out of the last mind right then, she saw Venetians rowing away across the lagoon on a still evening, Carpaccio's Venetians in doublet and hose, and they were Amedea and Gérard in the Carpaccio boat. Well, she concluded (but could not help looking out over the roofs, out to the dim lagoon, the grey tide-fall, for there, almost, almost, they rowed) I am a sentimentalist, in my housewifely way.

Venice's rituals were still performed, though often by different people. This was encouraging. And Francesca needed encouraging, even in her happiness now she needed it – because to plan a marriage and the raising of children on these befouled shoals, in this derelict civilisation, this museum, this tourist resort, was like planning them on a beached hulk. Guy knew that too, survivor of an empire and a love that he was. (They must go again to the Nilgiri Hills soon, make another effort to bring Viola Ashmanhaugh to spend her last years in Venice. But she did not want to leave the hills her husband had loved, cultivated, died in.) So it was pleasing to find familiar faces and affectionate voices when they went to the Do Mori for a glass of wine, and more than pleasing that last time everyone had drunk their health. Small things like that. Francesca dwelt on them, leaning against honeysuckle, hearing a gull croak, watching the twilight go grainier. Small things. Trudging along the Lido on stormy days. On blue evenings to scull the backwaters hour by hour. (Corrado could row his mother's old *s'ciopon* well now.) Regattas, exhibitions, concerts, restaurants, a movie with Huppert, something by Béjart's dancers . . . Guy and she did what all the friends and lovers and husbands and wives in the city did. And a few nights ago she had nearly understood what she needed to know, no, not know, feel.

Dawn in Venice had always been a ritual, and Guy and she were strolling home about dawn, by the Misericordia as it chanced. They stopped on the bridge where Ca' Tiepolo had stood till it was pulled down, where the Lezze palace still stood, sold by Amedea's family generations ago, which she used to pass on her way to her lover's attic along the quay. On the bridge they danced a few waltz steps. Venice was the same old floating heliopolis coming to light. Dancing, who would not dream she could feel the city stir at its warps, lilt and sway underfoot? And then for an instant Francesca thought she might learn from Gérard's miracle.

When he had held Amedea in his arms and waltzed on a bridge at daybreak, with his highest love and praise his soul had cried: This shall pass away. For an instant Francesca felt something of the exultation he had known, she was sure . . . And of what Amedea must have exulted in when she sensed that the love affair, in its lawlessness, in its abstraction, in its mutability, the love affair was the – oh, whatever grand thing she wanted.

Only for an instant. Guy and she were not souls to cry in victory: This shall pass away. Francesca realised that, at the next dance step. Their cry was: This shall endure. The more conventional cry, proved a lie by events time and again.

Well, she hoped their love – she used the conventional word in its most solid sense for their solid union – would last them out . . . still be declining quite fondly when they died. She expected it would. Just as Venice would still be declining not unattractively when as an old man Guy finished his last restoration job.

They stopped dancing and walked home.

Also by William Rivière

Watercolour Sky

'A first novel of great promise . . . a beautifully written, melancholy tale'
The Times

'A beautiful, strange, sometimes sinister idyll . . . Rivière is a specialist in haunting seascapes, creating a subtle and gripping story as if it were by Cotman or Crone'
John Bayley in the Evening Standard

Eros and Psyche

'A psychological work of great subtlety and penetration loosely based on a Greek myth and set on a lyrically described Greek island'
The Times

'Mesmerising . . . there are astonishing felicities'
Daily Telegraph

Borneo Fire

'A novel of an imaginative intensity, grandeur of conception, and moral seriousness, that sets it well apart from the common run of the English novel'
Scotsman

'Creates a compelling sense of the operations of fate . . . the country becomes material for Rivière's beautiful and evocative descriptions and his powerful story'
The Times Literary Supplement

Echoes of War

'Outstanding . . . *Echoes of War*, the story of a Norfolk land-owning family and their friends and connections, covers the first half of the century. It is a very ambitious and rich novel, the type of book that takes possession of your imagination'
Allan Massie in the Daily Telegraph Books of the Year

'Haunting . . . this novel has so much – psychological insight, descriptive brilliance, narrative skills'
Spectator

SCEPTRE